The Power of Two

Lori J. Sawicki

Praise for *The Power of Two*
2013 Midwest Book Award Finalist

"As a member of the Kindle Book Review Team, I've reviewed a lot of books. So, when I say that *The Power of Two* is the best book I've reviewed so far, this statement should not to be taken lightly. This is a great book. I'd recommend it to anyone, but particularly to girls feeling stuck in those middle years, wondering if anyone will ever see them for who they truly are." Lisa Runge, Kindle Book Review Team

"This book is wonderful! Everything about it is worth reading. It shows the importance of friendship and family and touches on serious issues that young people are forced to deal with. It's appropriate for anyone, young or young at heart." Marlena Hand, Author Alliance Book Review Team

"*The Power of Two* is a lyrical, powerful story about bullying, grief, and loss that will stay with you long after the last word is read. Readers of all ages will appreciate the story's wisdom and Sawicki's ability to capture the loneliness and fear of being an outcast. The characters practically walk off the pages and you'll be cheering and crying along with them. *Power* deserves a wide audience. Highly recommended!" Erin Fanning, author of *The Curse of Blackhawk Bay* and *Yarn Weavers*

"This book confirms my interest in encouraging adults to include children's fiction on their personal reading selections to experience and to be reminded of life events from an adolescent's point of view. This book exposes readers to a higher literary level. Sawicki holds the reader's attention by using characters, settings, and events that represent true to life experiences." Midwest Book Awards, Judge

Other books by Lori J. Sawicki

Because Sometimes a Miracle is a Pussy Willow Tree

When Truth Puts Its Shoes On

DEDICATION

To my husband, Chuck.
Partner extraordinaire. Staunch supporter.
Unconditional ally. Love of my life.

Contents

ACKNOWLEDGMENTS

This book launches the Identity Novels collection, and it couldn't have happened without the help of many people—all of whom I want to thank here.

C. Hart, elementary school counselor in Houston, who used *The Power of Two* as a group counseling tool. Her expert input and the subsequent phone call from the girls who read the book gave me critical information for revising the manuscript.

Maria Romero, who read this book years ago and gave me important feedback from the sixth-grade perspective.

Alison Robison, editor and mentor, who gave me important feedback from a sixth-grade teacher's perspective.

Erin Fanning and Natalie Aguirre, writers I met through The Society of Children's Book Writers and Illustrators, who, unfailingly, provide honest and constructive critiques of all my work.

Meghan Marsac, clinical psychologist, whose expert knowledge about child behavior was very helpful.

Lucas Romero, website creator, who helped establish and develop the Identity Novels site.

And my husband, Chuck, and son, Nathan, whose support is never ending. Their collaboration, insight, and advice were invaluable in defining and launching Identity Novels. www.identitynovels.com

Chapter 1
Queen of Sixth Grade

I had a plan. But it was risky. And I was pretty sure it would turn out just like my Aunt Judy's triple layer chocolate cake. A disaster. That cake looked good from the outside with a lot of thick frosting, but it tasted awful. When it came time to eat, everyone stayed away from it, like it had a disease.

I knew if I wasn't careful, I could end up the same. Because girls in the middle didn't make the plans or change things around. Being in the middle meant nobody noticed you—like in your class picture, where everyone's crammed together on the bleachers and nobody can see your face. I felt like that. You could barely see mine.

But I knew I had to try…the day Sadie proved she ruled the universe and could do whatever she wanted. The day I watched her bully Pru Wheeler in front of everyone, and I didn't say a word.

"I'm making new rules for Tower Tag," Sadie said in her queen voice. The Too Cool Club—the TCs for short—followed behind her like we always did. "It's too easy to capture me, so I want the guardians to block off the slides. That way, the warriors have to use the rope ladders to get to the tower."

Sadie talked about her new rules, and all the girls bobbed their heads, agreeing like they always did.

Inside, where no one could see, I rolled my eyes.

Tower Tag ranked right up there with stupid games, but we'd played it forever. The wooden jungle gym at school made the perfect fort, with the tower up high in the center of everything. That's where the guardians defended the commander from the warriors. And of course, Sadie always had the commander position. She owned it.

I hated Tower Tag because Sadie didn't play fair. No one else got to be the commander. And, for sure, no one else got to make the rules. But mostly, I hated it because Sadie excluded a lot of girls. If she decided you weren't cool, you didn't play.

"Can I be a watchman tomorrow?!" Amy asked, pleading for the best job.

"We'll see." Sadie flashed a smile at Tangerine, her best friend, whose real name was Tina but who Sadie thought needed a cool nickname. "If Tangerine doesn't want it, maybe you can have it."

Amy gave a hopeful sigh.

Dressed in the red Nike jacket she wore to school every day, her black hair in braids with red ribbons, Sadie looked like some kind of pro athlete getting ready for the big game. She had that instant cool—queen of the world—and could pull it off like no other sixth grader. She commanded attention. And as we walked toward the building, she had it from all the TCs. Except me.

I stopped listening to Sadie for a while and thought about my plan instead, not sure I had enough guts to go through with it. Because being a part of the TCs meant you went along. You never said what you really thought, and you never disagreed with Sadie. And my plan wasn't about following. It was about changing.

I tuned back in to Sadie when her easy-breezy tone changed to a red-alert. "Oh god, look at the brainiac."

Pru Wheeler was on the ground next to the picnic table where she read during every recess. She had her hands out, feeling around in the grass. After Sadie declared Pru uncool because it was lame to read so much, the TCs found it easy to ignore her. Plus, being the tiniest girl ever in the history of sixth grade didn't help. Pru spent a lot of time by herself.

Sadie stopped, and we all stopped. Then, she took an extra step, planting her feet right in front of Pru.

"Don't move. Please don't move," Pru said, leaning in close to the grass, patting it with both palms. Then, she looked up at us, blinking fast. "Can you see it?" she asked.

"Looks like you lost something there, Pru." Sadie's voice was filled with yuck, layered with sweet. A little like my Aunt Judy's cake.

"My contact lens. It popped out." She kept patting the ground. "Can you help me?"

Her hands moved over the grass, like she'd done this before, her little fingers searching around for the lens. The gold ring she wore had a pretty, purple stone. She squinted hard, eyes close to the ground. Brown hair, cut in a bowl shape, fell in her face.

Sadie looked at the TCs with a grin that always made my heart stumble, and I never felt sure I'd catch it before it landed in my stomach and made me want to throw up.

"Well, I don't know," she said. "Ms. Woods will kill us if we're late."

"Okay. Thanks anyway."

I didn't know many sixth graders who wore contacts—well, I didn't know any—and I doubted she'd ever find a little piece of plastic in all that grass. Not even if we all bent down to look. But no one moved to help her. Sadie hadn't given the go-ahead. She watched like Pru was a TV show.

I thought maybe we really should help Pru because you couldn't ignore a contact lens like you could a lost piece of Bubble Yum or a quarter. And besides, it felt wrong to just stand and stare at her. So, while my stomach re-scrambled all the eggs I had for breakfast, I knelt down to look.

"Thanks, Jamie," she said, giving me a quick nod.

Things got quiet then, and I knew Sadie was staring at me. It's funny how I could feel her anger stabbing me in the back, but I kept looking. And then she moved again, a Sadie-shadow stretching out over the grass making it hard to see—like ink, covering everything in black.

"Don't move too much," Pru said, and the TCs went completely silent. No one gave Sadie orders.

But Sadie ignored her and stepped sideways. Whenever Pru moved, Sadie moved—just enough to keep a shadow in Pru's way. Some of the girls giggled; Pru seemed panicked.

I was about to give up, when I saw a sparkle in the grass. Something shiny, like a big raindrop—just beyond Pru's left hand. But when I started to exclaim that maybe I'd found it, Sadie's black shadow moved in over us, and her Nike tennis shoe stepped down on the clear little circle.

A few of the TCs gasped. "*Sadie*," one of them said, her voice shocked but sort of excited. After that, they all started to whisper—hushed and secretive, like they were in awe of what she'd done.

But I wasn't in awe. Being part of the TCs didn't make me a mean girl. And I could barely breathe. So, I stayed on my hands and knees, trying to get air, wanting to pretend I hadn't seen. But, when I gave a quick look up, Sadie smirked at me. She knew I'd seen it all, and that smirk double-dared me to say something.

I shivered. All over. Then I stood, wiping at my jeans, so I wouldn't have to look at her anymore. She knew I wouldn't tell. The queen of the world had done an evil thing, and she'd get away with it like she always did.

"Well, you're not gonna find it," Sadie announced, and the TCs nodded like a bunch of bobbleheads. They moved in close around her. "It's gone." She retied the ribbon on one of her braids. "Sorry Pru. Guess you won't be able to finish studying—well, for whatever you're studying for."

The TCs laughed. I stood to the side, my stomach doing a cartwheel, about to crash.

Pru stopped patting the surface of the grass, then stood, too. She blinked and winked, but she stared straight at Sadie. "Oh I wasn't studying." Pru felt for her book on the picnic table. "I wanted to finish re-reading this. It's my favorite." She held out *The Complete Works of Robert Frost.*

A little part of me wanted to cheer because Pru stayed cool. She didn't dance like a Sadie-puppet.

But Sadie's eyes narrowed into little slits. "Robert Frost? That's lame. Great way to spend recess—reading a book about a famous painter."

Pru scrunched up her tiny face. "He's not a painter. He's a *poet*."

I don't think Pru meant it as a put-down. She just seemed surprised—that someone wouldn't know Robert Frost. But Pru's comment made Sadie look stupid. And boy, what a mistake. No one *ever* got away with making Sadie Levine look stupid.

Sadie's face became a volcano, kind of sputtering, about to erupt. But then, she smiled and tossed her head, her braids whipping out behind her. "You're a loser, Pru Wheeler," she said, moving away. The girls followed behind. "You've got L.S. Loser Syndrome."

I dropped back and let the TCs walk in front of me, watching how we kept playing follow the leader. I wondered if everyone considered Pru a loser. I'm pretty sure I didn't.

And right then, I knew it was time. The day had been coming like a thunderstorm you hear from your bed at night, far off but getting closer. I'd waited for it, feeling like I might explode. The time had come to try out my plan, though I knew it wouldn't be easy. And I'd need some luck. Sadie had the commander position, both in the tower and on the ground. So, it meant taking a big risk. And like I said, I could end up an outsider—a disease, like my Aunt Judy's cake.

Lori J. Sawicki

Chapter 2
Loser Syndrome

Tuesday morning, I decided to test my plan just before recess, when the TCs stood with Sadie at her locker. She checked her red cell phone, then put it in her pocket and pulled out some lip gloss—rolling it on her lips without a mirror. It smelled like bubble gum.

I watched them at locker A-12 for a long time. Some of the girls tried to look like Sadie, their hair in braids, too. Some stood so close, they practically stepped on her. Hands shot up all around.

"Pick me today, Sadie!" "No, no, me!"

The TCs zipped their jackets and waited for assignments. Sadie stood in the middle of it all, deciding everyone's position for the day.

Sadie's rule had lasted a long time. One girl in control for five years!—telling everyone what to do. And we let her. We followed her around like little kids after the ice cream truck.

And I wanted it to stop. I wanted my plan to change things a little. But like I said, it was risky. Dad always said you didn't rock the boat without making a lot of big waves, and he was probably right. For sure, Sadie would try to drown me in them. Because she knew how to twist the truth into something it wasn't, and I couldn't predict which way she'd twist mine.

I grabbed my jacket, thinking I had the courage today to do it. So, with a deep breath, I shut my locker and walked over to A-12. Sadie stood there, all serious, like choosing warriors and guardians ranked right up there with the president declaring war or something.

I interrupted the morning duty call. "Hi."

When no one noticed me, I cleared my throat and said, "Hey, does anyone want to play soccer today? I thought we could ask the girls from Mrs. Nila's class to start a game with us." I looked at Sue Ann—the closest thing I had to a friend. But she didn't turn my way. "Ms. Woods said we could use the ball and nets."

No one answered. The girls stared at Sadie, their eyebrows raised up in hope. And Sadie kept talking. Every once in a while, someone whispered, "Yes!" when Sadie assigned her a good position.

Not sure if anyone heard me, I tried again. "Anyone want to play soccer today?" No one even glanced around to see who'd asked.

But Sadie heard me. And I'll say one thing about her. She's not stupid. I think she understood right away what I wanted to do. That's why she pointed at me and said, "And Jamie, *you* can be a tower watchman today—with Sue Ann." She smiled, and all the girls gasped, like I'd been given a million dollars. Sue Ann finally looked at me, her eyes begging me not to play soccer. Being watchman meant you got to be in the tower with *her*, Commander Sadie. Definitely the place to be.

What a dilemma. I could take a risk or take the position, which Sadie didn't give to me often. I could be in the inner circle. The in-in circle. Sadie waited for me to decide. She knew she'd creamed the soccer idea.

"Okay," I said.

I'd chickened out and joined the girls for another recess of Tower Tag. And the next day, Sadie did it again.

"Jamie," she said, in that sweet layer voice—like Aunt Judy's chocolate frosting with the yuck underneath. "You can be up top with me again today. And *you* can pick the other watchman."

The quiet was loud. I'd just been made a *decision maker*—a gift from the leader of the world; a present everyone wanted to open, except me. Sadie might be smart, but you could see through her if you looked hard enough. I knew that red-alert in her eyes. She didn't like that I wanted to start something new.

As the quiet got bigger, I remembered Pru. Thinking about the contact lens made me feel prickly all over—like the TCs were becoming a thick, itchy sweater that didn't fit right anymore. And being made watchman two days in a row didn't make me want to keep wearing it.

"Actually, Sadie," I said, sucking in what seemed like the last bit of air in the hall. "I'm going to ask some of the girls from Mrs. Nila's class to play soccer today." A few of the TCs turned to me with real surprise, but mostly, everyone ignored me, including Sue Ann. "Do you guys want to join me?"

Sadie stopped and gave me the longest look in the history of sixth grade, like she might be trying to figure something out. Then she smiled—sort of. Her mouth gave a little quiver. And let me say, she looked like a monster in the movie right before it eats one of the heroes.

"I don't get it." She tipped her head sideways and scrunched up her nose. "Why do you want to do that?"

Well, I had a hundred reasons: I didn't want to follow rules I didn't make; I was sick of agreeing when I didn't; and I felt bad excluding kids just because Sadie thought they weren't cool. It was a good list, but girls in the middle couldn't be that honest—and, for sure, not to Sadie Levine. So, I kept it to myself.

"Well, I just thought it would be fun," I said. "You know, do something different for a change. Get a big group of girls to play. Just to try something new."

Sadie kept scrunching up her face then shook her head all puzzled and confused—like I was doing something wrong. She looked at the TCs. They looked at her, then at me. I could tell she was working on the twist.

Finally, she said, "Don't you want to be friends with us anymore?"

And there it was. Making what I said into something else—different from what it was. Twisting up the truth into a big, tangly knot. How did I answer that, when it had nothing to do with my real words? I just wanted to play soccer and ask some other girls to join us. I felt my face burn hot. TC eyes stared at the girl in the middle.

"Sadie!" I said, wanting her to know that wasn't it at all. "What do you mean? Of course I want to be friends. I just thought doing something new would be fun." And that was true. I sure didn't want to stop being friends with the TCs.

"It doesn't sound like it," Sadie said, folding her arms across the big NIKE logo on her jacket. She leaned back against her locker. Some of the other TCs folded their arms, too.

"Just because I want to play soccer with Mrs. Nila's class doesn't mean I—"

But Sadie shook her head. "Sounds like you're trying to ditch us."

The silence was louder than the train that ran by the

school every morning. It wasn't often all the TCs shut up at the same time. But they did now. And the noise was huge. It felt heavy. Even with all my planning, I never expected this.

"I'd never ditch you guys." I said it fast, trying to fix the moment before it could blow up into something worse. But I was too late.

"I think you are." Sadie stopped talking, so all the TCs could agree with her. And after they did, she said, "Go ahead and ask Maddie and Gwen to play soccer." The words came out slow and careful. "I'm sure they'd love to chase the ball around with you—right after they finish sucking their thumbs and playing on the teeter-totter." All the TCs laughed, and cold chills moved down the back of my legs. "Girls with Loser Syndrome should stick together."

It was out of control, and I didn't have a chance. Sadie had twisted and turned all my words, pulling the knot tight. Maybe never to be undone. The girl in the middle was about to become a TC black sheep.

"Come on you guys," Sadie said, with that creepy smile. "Jamie wants to hang out with some other girls, and that's okay with me." She said it in a sing-song voice, like having other friends besides the TCs wasn't allowed. And they left for the Tower, leaving me by myself in the hall.

Did you ever want to take something back the

minute you said it—like when you're a little too mouthy to your parents or you blame your sister for something you know she didn't do?

Standing there by myself, outside A-12, I felt hot and cold, thinking that I wanted to go backward—to turn the clocks back like at daylight savings time. You get an extra hour in the fall. Well, I would've been happy with two minutes. My plan had bombed. And over so fast! I could taste Aunt Judy's cake in the back of my throat.

When Mrs. Nila's class didn't come out for recess, I kicked the soccer ball around by myself. And I tried to be okay with what I'd done, but things just got worse after that. By lunchtime, most of the TCs ignored me. And after one whole day, they acted like they didn't know me at all. I wasn't sure I could last. It surprised me, how being in the middle of something you hated could suddenly feel a whole lot better than being alone.

Lori J. Sawicki

Chapter 3
The Tiniest Girl in Sixth Grade

I came home Wednesday after school feeling like I had L.S. stamped on my forehead. Boy, it didn't take much to become an outcast. I'd been friends with the TCs since second grade, but in the end, that didn't matter. The girls turned against me because Sadie had. Simple as that.

I wanted to talk to my mom about what I'd done. It seemed like her specialty. She spent a lot of time discussing 'office politics' at the dinner table whenever we found time to eat together, and Sadie and the TCs felt sort of like what she described.

If only I could catch her. My mom was like one of those high-powered, successful women you sometimes saw on the cover of a magazine or in a movie. Her cell phone rang as soon as she got out of bed in the morning until she kissed me good night, and I don't think she really saw me most days. If you weren't quick enough, she could slip away—'sucked into the wonders of hand-held technology,' my dad said sometimes. But I thought I'd try.

I moped around waiting for her, flopped out on my bed, staring at the ceiling. Just when I decided I'd made a big mistake, my sister, Maxine, came home. She dumped her hundred pound backpack on the foyer floor, then came upstairs.

"Hey, Tweeter," she said, using the old nickname she still loved and I still hated. She passed my door, hurrying down the hall with her cell phone pasted to her ear. I barely saw her as she blurred by. I couldn't hear the whole conversation, but she talked about her play and how Mom needed to take in the costumes. "I can't be Juliet in these dresses! Whoever wore them before must've been huge. I swear, the gowns are like a size 18 or something!"

I rolled my eyes and reached over to the drawer of my nightstand. I took out my spiral notebook and a pencil. On a fresh, white page, I wrote:

> OUT!
> It isn't easy being in.
> But it's harder to be out.
> Changing things can wreck your life
> That's what 'change' is all about.
> Learning how you want to be
> Takes a lot of energy
> Might find yourself kicked out
> Makes you wonder, makes you doubt
> If being you is worth the risk
> Knowing you might not be missed.
> Jamie C.

"Hey, Tweets," my sister called. "Canya come here a sec?!"

The Power of Two

I pulled myself off the bed and wandered down the hall. Standing in the doorway of my sister's room, I watched her pose in front of the mirror giving a frantic frown at the velvet dress she had on. Maxine had the tall and thin thing going, with long blond hair that she straightened with a hot iron but was really curly when she left it alone.

My hair was nothing like hers—except for the color. I'd cut mine short because it was too frizzy to do anything with it. And my bangs were always falling in my face. For sure, I was a loser in the hair department.

But people stared at Maxine when she walked by. Her hair could sway back and forth or bounce. She'd probably make a good Juliet, but I didn't tell her. I figured she already knew.

"Tweets, *where* is the sewing basket? It's always in the spare bedroom, but it's not there!" She said it like the basket had been moved on purpose to make her life miserable.

"I think it's downstairs in the den. Mom was fixing your jeans last night."

"Will you run down and get it?" She pulled the dress off over her head and asked without it really being a question. She knew I'd do it. I'd been her faithful servant since birth. "I need to pin the bottom of this one, so Mom'll know where to hem it." She talked more to herself than to me.

But I didn't move. I didn't hurry away like I usually did. And when Maxine tossed the dress on her bed, she scrunched up her eyebrows and gave me an extra-long look. "What's with you? You're all glum."

Her question surprised me. Maxine gave her life a lot of attention, and she rarely looked past the mirror to see mine. I shrugged. To be honest, I wanted to cry, knowing I'd made myself an outcast at school, and no one cared.

"Tweets, what's the deal? And will you go find it?" I decided she didn't really want to hear my problems, so I went downstairs to get the basket.

Just then, my parents walked in. Dad hung the car keys on the hook in the closet, and Mom put her briefcase down by the door. "Hi Jamie," they said at the same time.

"Hi. Listen Mom, can I ta—"

"And another thing." My mom waved a hand around like she was batting at a fly. "Mike completely ruined the photos for the ad. We have to reshoot all of them." Mom rushed by me to the kitchen, and I pulled back to let her pass. She opened the fridge door and then freaked. "Oh no. We're out of Diet Coke! Jamie!" She put her hands on her hips. "Will you write Diet Coke on the grocery list!?"

"There's some in the garage," I said, in a normal

voice, and my mom jumped. She seemed surprised to see me there. I went to the fridge in the garage and got her a can, then grabbed three more, just in case. Back in the kitchen, I handed one to her. She took it without looking my way. "You saved me." She popped the top, talking to Dad while she drank. "I swear he took the pictures at night!"

Mom rushed past me, unbuttoning her blouse as she climbed the stairs to their room. Dad followed behind, pulling at his tie. "I'm going to have to work all weekend to get this fixed." I heard a loud sigh as she finished the climb and then she exclaimed, "Oh, Honey! That dress is *beautiful* on you. What great fabric!"

I stood in the foyer, sewing box in hand, listening to them. After stopping off in Maxine's room, they went on to their own. I heard Dad say that he'd have to put in extra time over the weekend, too, showing properties to some 'A-list clients.' As owner of Corman Real Estate, Dad felt he needed to handle the deals himself. I decided that discussing my problems with Tower Tag should probably wait.

That night, I wrote another poem.

SUNFLOWER SISTER

You are a sunflower
Tall and bright
Light follows you.

I am lost
In your shade
The sun doesn't find me.
No one sees me
I have no color
While you blaze
Yellow-bright.

Jamie C.

****

The next morning, I sat at the kitchen table staring into my bowl of Lucky Charms like it was some kind of crystal ball. But I couldn't find answers in there. A bunch of soggy marshmallows couldn't help me, even if some of them were four-leaf clovers.

Maxine breezed in. Her long hair swished back and forth as she walked around the kitchen. I watched how easy she moved, how it seemed the day had been waiting for her to appear. "What's up, Tweets?" She gave me a quick look. But when I didn't answer, she shrugged and punched numbers into her phone. "Ellen, hey, it's me." She turned away and pulled a Pop-Tart from the box on the counter, tossing it into her backpack. Her energy made me tired. I just wanted to skip school and go back to bed.

All morning, I sat through class dreading recess, and when Ms. Woods excused us, I got my jacket and stood with my back to locker A-12. After Sadie finished choosing teams, she said in an extra-loud voice, "And let's not wait for Jamie. I'm sure she wants to play soccer with her new L.S. friends." The TCs laughed, and Sadie slammed her locker door. I turned around and watched them follow her outside.

What a horrible walk to the soccer field. My stomach felt like a tetherball, going around and around, flung back and forth, and no matter how many deep breaths I took, I couldn't get it to stop. I waited for Mrs. Nila's class to come out, but they didn't, so I was alone again to play soccer by myself.

But just when I thought I might be sick, my insides dizzy and scared, the day changed. Like when the sun finds an open slot in a sky full of clouds and sneaks out, shining down in those long rays. Sort of a surprise. And sometimes surprises change your life.

Wearing jeans and a University of Michigan sweatshirt, Pru walked over and said the weirdest thing: "Looks like you could use some help."

And that's when I officially met the tiniest, strangest person in sixth grade—one of those quiet kids from class; not someone you ever talk to; and easy to miss. She was so little! But she came into my life in a big way, like an explosion that set off the blast that changed my life in the middle forever.

Lori J. Sawicki

Chapter 4
An Offer to Help

I turned around, and there she stood, this girl I barely knew. I swear, Pru could hide in your shadow or turn sideways and disappear. She smiled at me, then frowned, blinking and winking. She popped out a contact lens onto her finger.

Staring at her, I didn't know what to say, so I blurted out my first thought. "Why don't you just get glasses?"

I didn't mean to sound rude. It's just that contacts seemed so fussy and like they would, well, pop out a lot. But Pru, in what I'd think of later as her Pru-way, said a funny thing. "They make me look extra mousy."

I tried not to laugh because she did kind of look like a mouse—I mean with her being so tiny. And the way she wore her brown hair, pushed behind her ears. Not that she had whiskers or anything, but she seemed kind of soft. And I think Pru had it right: glasses would've made her look more like one.

"I'm Prudence by the way." She put out her hand to shake mine, acting like I didn't know her from class or hadn't tried to help find her contact lens. But I'd been a Sadie-follower, never really trying to talk to her. "Prudence Wheeler. People just call me Pru." She said this with a wheezy sound in her throat.

Introducing myself seemed silly, but I shook her hand anyway—I didn't want to be impolite. But how *weird* could she be? She didn't act like anybody I'd ever met. "I'm Jamie, uh, Corman," I said.

Pru nodded. Short. Quick. "I know. You're one of the popular girls." She said this with the contact still on the tip of her finger. "Thanks for trying to help me find my lens the other day."

I had two thoughts at the same time: One, anyone who considered me popular had to be crazy. Two, the contact definitely needed water.

"Shouldn't you get that in something?" I pointed, watching it start to shrivel up on her finger. I didn't know much about contacts, but I was pretty sure they needed to be wet.

Pru popped the lens back into her eye, blinking it into place. When she finished, she looked at the soccer ball, then at me. "So, do you need some help?"

"Help doing what?" I said, surprised by her question.

"Well, I heard you ask the girls if they wanted to play soccer. And no one did. So, I figured you might need some help making your plan work."

I wondered if it was possible for Pru to read my

mind. "The plan?" I tried to look confused. "What plan?"

Pru glanced over her shoulder at the play structure. "Getting them to do something else." She said it like she understood my problem exactly. When I didn't answer, she went on. "You guys play that Tower game every day. It sounded like you were tired of it." She paused. Taking a breath seemed hard.

I stared at her, my mouth hanging open like a flytrap—something my grandma used to say. "Well, aren't you?" she asked.

"What?"

"Tired of it?"

I shrugged, not sure I should tell that kind of truth to someone I didn't know, but I did anyway. "I guess so."

Then Pru said something I sure didn't expect. "And tired of her?"

Pru's tiny brown eyes seemed really big right then. She looked at me like I might be a bug or creepy crawly caught in a jar. In less than three minutes, she'd summed up my whole sixth-grade life. "Not that Sadie's a bad person," Pru said. "I just think she needs a lot of attention. And the other girls...well...they probably haven't developed enough self-esteem yet to say no to her."

I don't think I said a word for almost a minute. Because who talked like that in sixth grade? I felt pretty sure I didn't know what 'developing self-esteem' meant, and it seemed she'd read every poem I'd ever written about my problems with the TCs. Somehow, Pru knew me, without knowing me at all.

I decided not to be too honest. "Well," I said. "I like to play soccer."

Pru gawked at me, her eyes pushing into mine. "Really?" The word came out like 'rhheeeeeeelhhhyy,' a scratchy sound in her lungs making the 'e' start with an 'h.' "I thought you liked to write poetry."

I frowned. How could she possibly know that? No one had ever seen my poetry notebook, and only once had I shown Mom and Dad some of my work. They'd been pretty bored with it—Mom giving a quick, "That's nice, Honey," and Dad a sleepy, "Good job." I guess they weren't much to read. So, I kept my love for writing poems a deep, Jamie-secret.

"I see you in class sometimes," she said, her voice easy, except for the wheezing. "When we're supposed to be taking notes. Sometimes you write a poem instead."

I thought about where Pru sat. From her desk, she could probably see me writing poems instead of working, even though I thought I hid it pretty well. But what did *she* do during class? Spy on me? It seemed a whole lot like snooping.

And just when I thought I wanted to be mad at this girl, for barging into my life, thinking I needed help, and then being a snoop on top of it all, she said another surprising thing. "I'd love to read your poetry sometime, you know, if you ever wanted an opinion or just someone to share with."

For sure now, I would've won the contest for the longest time without speaking. She seemed nice enough—friendly. But what sixth grader talked like a college professor and came crashing into your life, knowing everything about you? Pru Wheeler was different, but she didn't seem to notice or care. And when I didn't answer, she just asked me the question again.

"Do you want some help?"

"Sure." I couldn't think of anything else to say.

"Okay, because I might have an idea."

Lori J. Sawicki

Chapter 5
Sixth-Grade Disease

Pru told me her idea the next day when an amazing thing happened: She invited me to her house after school.

And what a relief. Because my life as a TC was over. In just one day, nobody wanted me around, including Sue Ann. It hadn't taken much. Just one suggestion to change things a little—and I was out. Choosing not to play Tower Tag had turned me into an official sixth-grade disease. For sure, I was just like my Aunt Judy's cake.

I felt it most during Book Time, when Ms. Woods let us sit on the floor and read. The TCs wouldn't let me into our usual circle on the carpet.

"There's not enough room," Sadie said, scooching over toward Sue Ann. She gave me an innocent smile, and Sue Ann pretended to read.

They could've made room. They could've fit five more Jamies into the circle. But Sadie stared at me, and the rest of the TCs stared at me, too.

I did my best to sound cool. Sure of myself. "I could squeeze in." I nodded at the space between Sue Ann and Taylor.

"There isn't *room*." Sadie's voice rose to red-alert. If she said it again, Ms. Woods might look up from her desk.

Oh, I wanted to be invisible—a ghost or some fog that could disappear. So I didn't have to watch them watch me. I felt like the dog that's been at the Humane Society for weeks. The one nobody wants. It's not cute enough or cool enough to keep for a lifelong friend, and so people just walk away. But in my case, I'd be the one walking.

Only, how? I stood there, my mouth dry like I'd eaten too many pretzels. I wanted to say something—to show Sadie I didn't care. Something funny to wipe away her smug smile. But those pretzels wouldn't let me talk.

I shrugged and pretended it didn't matter. But it did. I left the carpet knowing I'd been officially kicked out of the TCs.

I glanced over at Pru, who always sat by herself during Book Time, but it didn't feel right to just go over and plop down next to her, like I'd picked her second over my so-called friends. But after I went to a corner near the windows and ducked down behind my book, wanting to cry, Pru came and sat down next to me.

She didn't make a big deal of it, and I pretended not to notice. But a few minutes later, she slid a note to me.

The Power of Two

Want to come to my house after school? I can tell you my idea.

Once I got over my surprise, I smiled and gave her a quick nod.

When the last bell rang, I used Pru's cell phone to call my mom. And even though she sounded impatient that I'd interrupted her important meeting, she gave me permission to walk home with her.

"Call Maxine to pick you up when you're done," she said.

So, I went to Pru's house on Friday, a couple weeks before spring break. At first, we didn't say much. We hadn't become best friends or anything, and we couldn't just start talking like we'd known each other forever. But Pru, in her usual Pru-way, made things easy. "So I have this idea about how to change the dynamics of our sixth-grade girl leadership."

Right then, I wanted a dictionary because I wasn't exactly sure what 'dynamics' were. She talked like she'd gone to college. "Okay," I said, trying not to show that I didn't get it. "What?"

"Well," she said, with that strange wheezing sound—like she had an extra bad cold that was hanging on a long time. "Maybe you should try something different. Not soccer."

"Why?"

"It's so common," she said. "Everybody plays it. Have you seen how many teams there are for Wheatland Saturday Soccer?" She didn't wait for an answer. "If you want to change the direction of things, you should put something new out there—a little more unique. It'll make your plan more interesting."

"Like what?"

"How about lacrosse? I could teach you."

"What's lacrosse?"

"It's a game sort of like soccer, where you try to get a ball into a net. Only you use sticks. My brother plays for the University of Michigan." Pru's breath seemed caught in her chest. "I think we could get people interested in something that's different. Especially the boys. Then, the girls might want to play, too." She fussed with her contact again, rubbing her eye, blinking fast.

"Maybe it'll help them," she went on, "to stop handing their power over to Sadie."

I walked along beside her, not understanding a word of it, wondering if she'd given me the whole plan. None of it made much sense. I didn't know how you *got* power in the first place, and if you had it, how you gave it to someone else. And I sure didn't get how lacrosse would fix it.

When we got to Pru's house, two boys came running out. They grabbed bikes from the garage and raced off together. "My brothers Kyle and Dane," she said. Neither had bothered to shut the door.

We went inside, and I heard voices. Older. They came from upstairs, and the sound echoed around their very big house, bouncing back and forth like in a museum. Pru pointed to the second floor and put her backpack in the closet. I put mine in there with it. "Two other brothers, Blair and Chris."

I followed her down a long hall, noticing all the clothes. They were flung over furniture and in piles, and coats hung on doorknobs. Sports equipment filled every corner, backpacks sat dumped on the stairway, and there were so many shoes! I bet at least fifty pair— mostly tennis shoes. Thrown everywhere.

We went into the kitchen, and the fridge was open, an arm resting across the top of the door. Before I could sit down, a head popped out around the side, and Pru's face lit up—it shined like sun on water. "Marty!" she squealed. I don't think I'd ever seen her smile.

Pru ran to him, and he picked her up like an armful of air. "Hi, Mouse." He gave Pru a twirl around and around. Finally, Marty let her down, and she turned to me with a face I'd come to think of as Marty-delight.

"Jamie, this is my brother, Marty." She turned back to him. "What are you doing home?" She turned back to me. "Here, sit down." She pointed toward a stool at a long counter. "I'll get some snacks."

"My classes finished early," he said. "I'm now officially on spring break." Marty gave a dramatic bow then gave Pru a big smile. "It's good to see you, Mouse. How's the cough?" They wore matching University of Michigan sweatshirts, and he looked just like Pru, only taller. They had the same color hair and eyes. But he had rosy cheeks, and there was nothing rosy about hers.

She shrugged, then nodded. "It's okay."

They had big warmth between them, moving like light being set free. A wave dancing around the kitchen. I liked watching it—they had a different relationship than my sister and me. It made me think I should write a poem about them.

"So what are you guys up to?" He really seemed interested, and he talked to me, too. I liked that about him. It felt strange to have a grown-up actually look me in the eye and wait for me to answer.

"I'm going to teach Jamie how to play lacrosse." Pru said this in a voice so sure, I could only turn to her and stare. "Would you help us, Marty? Can you practice with us this weekend?"

"Sure." He got up from his stool. "I'm going over to

see the guys right now, but why don't we start tonight. When I get back, we can run some drills in the backyard. Jamie, are you staying for supper?"

"Well, gosh, I don't know. I guess I could." Pru hadn't asked me to stay, but she nodded in agreement. "I'll have to call my mom."

"Cool," he answered. "I'll see you guys later then." And he left, giving his sister a kiss on the top of the head.

Pru grabbed two sodas from the fridge, and we went upstairs to her room on the second floor. Moving down another long hall to get there, we passed packages of toilet paper, Kleenex boxes, and tons more shoes. I had to step over them and around a large laundry basket. Dirty clothes spilled over the sides.

Pru opened the door to her room, and we walked into a field of flowers. It was completely different from the rest of the house. "Wow, this is really pretty," I said, looking around. The bottom half of each wall was painted light purple, the top part wallpapered in little violets. A purple quilt was spread out over a double canopy bed in the corner. Flowery pillows were everywhere. And under it all—purple carpet. Plus, the room was spotless. Pru shut the door, closing out the tornado on the other side.

The flowers surprised me. I mean, Pru didn't have that frilly, girly thing going, and she didn't wear makeup or lip gloss like half the girls in sixth grade. The Pru I saw every day wore jeans and a sweatshirt, and she never put barrettes or ribbons in her hair. She didn't seem fussy. But her bedroom seemed the opposite of the girl living in it, kind of a 'contradiction'—a word Maxine used a lot to describe some new guy she had a crush on. She liked to pretend her boyfriends were mysterious and complicated, when they acted pretty much like everybody else. But the word fit Pru. I'd learn she was a contradiction in a lot of ways.

A bookshelf as tall as the ceiling was filled with more books than I'd ever read in my whole life. On the wall next to it was a picture of a woman with her arm around Pru. Puppies sat at their feet. There were posters of Hillary Clinton and Johnny Depp behind her bed. I smiled inside. Pru was like two different people—a puzzle, really. "It's a lot prettier than my room," I said.

"Thanks. Purple's my favorite color."

Pru put the sodas on the nightstand and kicked off her shoes, grabbing a notebook and pencil from her desk drawer. Sitting cross-legged on the bed, Pru wrote numbers down the left side of the paper. I sat opposite her, waiting.

"We can work on our plan for lacrosse when Marty comes home tonight." She pushed strands of brown hair behind her ears. "So, let's start by listing what bothers you about Tower Tag."

The Power of Two

Pru seemed to know exactly what to ask and exactly what was wrong. In less than a week, she'd figured out my whole life. I stared at her, my mouth open, but no words came out. I had a feeling that if I stayed friends with Pru, I'd be speechless a lot.

Lori J. Sawicki

Chapter 6
The Truth about Lemmings

"Okay," I said, finally, not sure where to start. Because I had a lot of items for *that* list. "Well, number one, it leaves people out." I sighed. "I mean, Sadie has this little group, and she doesn't let other people in. So, lots of girls in class don't even get to play."

I realized as I said it, that Pru was one of those girls. Never picked. On the outside of the circle. I wanted to apologize, but she waved the pencil in the air, like she knew my thoughts.

"It's okay. Tower Tag never interested me," she said with a sniff. "And I never wanted to be in that group, anyway."

I watched her face, wondering if that's how she really felt. Did anyone feel okay being left out? But she just gave a Pru-nod and wrote down the entry on the list:

1. Excludes people

"Okay, what else?" She chewed the end of the pencil, waiting for me to go on.

I sprawled out length-wise on Pru's bed, her purple comforter soft and cushy beneath me. "Well, it's boring. That's for sure." Pru wrote that down. "*And* it's always the same leader." I hesitated, staring at the poster of Hillary Clinton. "No one else ever gets to be the boss except Sadie."

Pru wrote:

2. Uninteresting
3. Same leadership

Before I could stop myself, I said what had really bugged me for a long time. "The weird thing is that all the girls *let* her be the leader. Every day. They just follow along."

Pru smiled and gave a Pru-nod. "Yes. They've given up their power."

There it was again—the word 'power.' And still, I didn't understand. "You said that before. About power. And handing it over. What do you mean?"

Pru took a soda from the nightstand and handed it to me then took the other for herself. She looked around the room, and her eyes landed on the bookshelf. "Well, for example, I love to read." She popped open her soda and took a sip. "And Sadie thinks that's lame. So, in order to be friends with her, what if I decided not to read anymore?" She stared at me like I should totally get it.

"Yeah...." I dragged out the word, so she'd keep

talking and give me something more to go on.

"Well, if I did that—played Tower Tag instead of read, or I stopped reading altogether just because she wanted me to—she'd have the power." Pru took in a breath-wheeze. "The whole thing about power, is that I'd be giving mine up. To her."

"But power of what?" I still didn't get it.

"What *I* wanted to do. My life."

I thought about it, still not sure I understood. I opened my soda to stall for time, not wanting Pru to think I was a total idiot. Finally, I said, "So, you think all the girls have given up their power to Sadie?"

"A lot of it," Pru replied. "I mean, Jamie, do you think they *like* to play that game?"

"Well, yeah. Sure," I said, surprised. "They do it every day."

Pru's dark eyes seemed darker then. "Well, so did you. But you didn't like it. I bet practically all of them feel the same way you do—tired. Tired of it. But they don't know how to stop playing without making Sadie mad."

My mouth hung open again. "You really think so?"

"Mmmmm…" I got a Pru-nod. "I bet a few of them are a little jealous of you right now."

"Jealous of me?"

"Because you didn't play this week."

"Well, they can't be *that* jealous. No one's even talking to me."

"They're just afraid."

Pru sounded so wise, so sure. I wondered then how she got so smart—if reading all those books had helped her figure things out better than other people could. She seemed like a genius, and the way she talked made me wish I had that dictionary handy. "They've given up their power for so long," she went on, "they don't know how to get it back."

"Maybe it's stupid to want to keep it," I blurted out, knowing what I felt but not sure how to say it. "Because if keeping your power means all your friends are mad at you and not talking to you, what good is it?"

"It's a hard trade, for sure." Pru put the soda can back on the nightstand and had a giant coughing fit. It took her a while to settle down.

"Ugh," I said, rolling over to stare at the ceiling. "I'm just tired of being a lemming all the time." I repeated the word Maxine used to describe someone following the crowd.

"Well, that's actually just a myth. Lemmings don't really follow each other to the end of cliffs and jump off together. But I know what you're saying." Her words came out in a big, long wheeze. "Really, though, I don't think anyone *wants* to be a conformist."

I got up and checked her bookshelf for a dictionary. I figured I might as well get it down and start reading. Or maybe I should just carry one with me if Pru and I were going to be friends.

"Well, maybe I do," I said, feeling grumpy. "Because not being one is lonely. And at least a lemming gets to be with a flock of other lemmings. It's not an outcast. A disease." I could taste my Aunt Judy's cake in my mouth.

Pru almost smiled. "You're not a lemming, Jamie. You're a poet. You have an independent spirit."

I sat back down and got quiet. I didn't know what an independent spirit was, but I knew I wanted to be a poet. And no one had ever understood me like Pru. In a few short days, she somehow knew me better than I knew myself.

"Okay. Anything else?" Pru leaned over and showed me the list.

1. Excludes people
2. Uninteresting
3. Same leadership
4. Creates conformists

"No. I guess that's it."

Pru tapped the pencil on the pad of paper. "So, what is it you wanted to accomplish?"

"Whatdoyamean?"

"Well, like a goal. Why did you want to play soccer? What did you really want to happen?"

I waited about five seconds, and then the words rushed out of me like I was a can of Sprite and Pru had shaken me up and popped me open. "I want things to be more fair. It's not right that Sadie's the boss over everybody—like we can't make our own decisions and don't have our own ideas. Girls shouldn't be excluded just because Sadie says they're not cool. I'm tired of following her around like, well, a *lemming.*" I sighed. "I feel like I'm stuck—that we're all stuck—with Sadie. And I'm sick of it. I guess that's it."

I should've added that I really just wanted to breathe. But I didn't think that would make much sense. It didn't make a lot of sense to me, but that's what I'd been feeling lately—like I couldn't get enough air.

Pru rubbed her eyelid. "Okay, so your first plan didn't work. What if this one doesn't either?"

"You mean, what if no one wants to play lacrosse?"

A Pru-nod. "If your friends keep playing Tower Tag and they still ignore you. Are you going be okay with that?"

I shrugged. "I don't know. I guess I'll have to be."

"Okay," Pru said, scribbling on the paper. "Then the real goal is for Jamie to be okay if *she* changes, even if no one else does."

Her words bothered me. I wasn't sure if that was the goal at all. Did I want to be okay alone? Without the TCs? That wasn't the original plan. I'd wanted things to change—a break from the way things were. Not to break *up* with them. I'd hoped that after Sadie got over being mad, the TCs would accept me back in. I stared at Pru, afraid that she'd just predicted my future—a future I wasn't sure I wanted.

Lori J. Sawicki

Chapter 7
Lacrosse!

Eating dinner at the Wheeler's was like being in a really loud restaurant with a lot of waiters. Mr. Wheeler brought pizza from the kitchen into the dining room where we all sat at a long table. Then, one brother popped up from his chair and brought back more sodas and extra napkins. And another disappeared to return with a second load of breadsticks and chicken wings. It was crazy around the dinner table, and I just sat there, not quite sure how to talk to Pru over all the noise.

As I listened to the sports talk, lacrosse scores, and kidding about girls, I wondered where Pru's mom was. No one mentioned her. And the table had no extra chairs—they'd pulled mine in from the living room. Finally, I leaned over to Pru and asked.

"Where's your mom?"

Through a bite of pizza, Pru said, "She died. Five years ago."

I stopped chewing on my breadstick, my throat closing up. "I—I'm sorry. Gosh, Pru. That's—well—that's awful."

"It's okay. Thanks."

She told me in her usual Pru-way—simple, calm.

But I couldn't finish eating. I put the breadstick down on my plate and took a quick sip of soda to clear out what felt like a hundred cotton balls in my throat. Maybe I didn't get as much time with my mom as I wanted, and maybe she had a crazy schedule, but I always believed she'd be there. Moms didn't leave. I mean, you could count on that, right? A shiver tiptoed down my arms.

"Dane, pass me a breadstick," Chris said from the far end of the table. Dane picked one up and launched it to him like a football. It hit Chris on the chin.

"Hey, throw me one." Blair put up his hands to catch a pass. Dane fired it across the table, and Blair snatched it from the air, holding it up like he'd scored a touchdown.

Marty pulled the breadsticks out of Dane's reach. "Enough guys. Jamie's gonna think we were raised in a cave."

"*You* were," Dane teased, biting into a chicken wing. "That's why you never have any dates." He talked with his mouth full.

That brought a lot of laughs, but Marty stayed cool. "Yeah, I traded in girls for good grades. At least I'm not flunking American History."

All the brothers said ooooooohh and then clapped. Blair gave Marty a high five. "Good one!"

I glanced over at Pru, wondering how she fit into all of this—her life as the only girl in an all-boy locker room. She seemed invisible, lost in the action and kidding around.

Mr. Wheeler broke up the joking. "Speaking of which, don't you have a paper due on the Declaration of Independence?" His face was serious.

The table quieted down, and Dane shrugged. "If I get a B on the paper, I can pull my grade up to a C+. Don't worry, Dad."

"But Mrs. Watson expects a lot."

Dane rolled his eyes and nodded, stuffing a breadstick into his mouth. "Tell me about it. She even wants us to include 'little known facts' in our report." He imitated a woman's voice, and everyone laughed again.

But just when it seemed that Pru had been lost in all the noise—lost, the way I sometimes felt around Maxine—she became visible again. "Then you should make sure you mention that the Declaration of Independence wasn't really signed on July 4, 1776."

She paused, chewing her pizza like she didn't notice the entire family had stopped talking. After a swallow of soda, she said, "The wording of the Declaration was approved on July 4, but it wasn't signed until August 2." She gave a Pru-glance at her brother and then finished off her Coke.

"Mouse is our resident encyclopedia," Dane said to me with a laugh. "Born with an IQ of, like, a million." But she had his attention. You couldn't ignore a person like Pru, especially when she had the key to a better grade.

"*Pru* has a deep interest in a lot of subjects," Marty said, obviously the only one in the family allowed to call her Mouse. "And Dane would be smart to listen up."

I wondered what it felt like to be the only girl in a family of boys—growing up without a mom. I mean, Pru could handle them. She proved that. But it seemed like swimming in the ocean without a boat to climb into when you got tired. Or being lost in the woods at night and no moon to help you find the way out. I'd never thought about my mom not being around.

After dinner, Marty took Pru and me to the backyard where he'd set up nets that looked like soccer nets. He carried three sticks with little baskets attached to each end, and a hard, yellow ball.

"Okay," he said, motioning for us to follow him. "The object of the game is to shoot the ball into the net, using a stick." He picked one up and handed it to me. "It's called a 'crosse.'" I took it, not sure what to do. But Pru just nodded and said, "He's really good at this."

"Now, Pru said you guys want to play this at recess, so I'm going to simplify the rules and teach you a scaled back version because you'll never have enough time for a regulation game." He paused and gave me a don't-worry smile. "I'll explain how you can play with just the two of you—you'll just have to do it without goalies."

Marty talked to us like adults. And even though I didn't understand everything he said, it was nice to be treated like that—smart enough to get it. It was easy to see why Pru loved him so much.

That night, Marty showed us how to use the sticks and carry the ball in the basket part called the 'pocket.' He explained the 'attackers,' the 'middies,' and the 'defenders' and their positions on the field. When I told Pru that it sounded a little like Tower Tag, she laughed so hard she started coughing. Marty finally handed her something he called an inhaler, and she put it to her mouth and squeezed. It looked sort of like sucking helium out of a balloon, so you can talk funny afterward. But I knew the inhaler wasn't a toy, and that Pru had more than just a cold.

After marking out a small field across the lawn with white chalk, Marty had us take turns playing different positions. He explained about the restraining box and the crease. And after a quick talk about penalties, he gave us safety goggles to put on and yelled, "Let's try it!"

Pru and I ran around with Marty for almost two hours, long after dark. Somebody in the Wheeler house eventually turned on the backyard floodlights, and I zipped up my jacket against the cold.

Holding the stick in my hand, I zigzagged a path across the Wheeler's back lawn, changing directions, making fast cuts and turns. I moved hard, pushing.

Marty spent a lot of time hollering things like, "You're *defending*! You need to be back by the net!" "No, no, you're attacking—you can't enter the crease!" And he played all the other positions, while we worked on just one or two.

Pru and I passed the ball back and forth, learning how to control it, flinging it through the air, dropping it. Cradling it. Sometimes my feet didn't feel the ground. Once, I seemed to fly. And even though I was tired and out of breath, I felt strong.

By the time Marty said we'd done enough for the night, we had the hang of it. He told us we'd given him quite a workout, and he wouldn't want to be in a match against us in a couple years. I could tell that made Pru feel good because she smiled at him and gave me a high five.

"Next time, we'll work on the face-off. But for now, you guys keep practicing your passes. You should also try playing goalie—learn how to protect the net."

Marty drove me home that night, and Pru and I sat in the backseat talking about our plan and how to get kids to play lacrosse with us. We felt sure when they saw how cool the game was, everyone would want to try it.

Later, before I went to bed, I wrote a poem in my spiral notebook. For the first time in the history of my entire life, I had a true friend.

Friendships
Here and gone
Lost and found
All my friends
Nowhere around.
But then one day
Pru walks in
And your life is never
The same again.
Jamie C.

That night, I realized being around someone like Pru helped you be more sure about yourself. Maybe because you spent more time *being* your real self than following other people around and acting like them.

Pru knew who she was. She walked alone, without many friends, but she seemed okay with it. And I thought maybe I wanted to know that path the way Pru did—even if it meant walking without the TCs. I wasn't sure how to do it, though. Because even with the good feelings I had about Pru, I knew lacrosse could be the beginning of something awful between me and the TCs.

Chapter 8
Saran Wrap

Monday at school, I didn't try to sit with Sadie and the TCs during Book Time. Instead, I just sat next to Pru on the floor near the fish aquarium. She smiled at me and nodded, scooching over to give me room.

Careful to not get caught, we wrote notes the entire half hour, hiding them under our hands and sliding them back and forth between us.

I ♥ lacrosse! I pushed the note slowly over to Pru while I pretended to read.

Me too! Pru wrote back. *I think we're good!* ☺

And then she had a coughing fit, and we had to wait for the kids and Ms. Woods to stop looking at her.

Finally, I wrote: **What's with your cough?**

I have asthma

Sorry! Is it bad?

Sometimes. I'm allergic to a lot of stuff, too

Like what?

Perfume, smoke, aspirin, peanuts. Even bees

Wow

Ms. Woods has an epi-kit in her desk for me

What's that?

Medicine, in case I get stung by a bee

Sorry

It's okay

I hope our plan works!

It will. But if it doesn't, we can play by ourselves! Ha ha ☺

I hoped we wouldn't have to do that because who wanted to spend recess playing a two-man game of lacrosse? We wanted others to join. To get the girls away from stupid Tower Tag and do something else. That's what Pru and I were doing, right? Trying to change things?

I guess I wasn't sure anymore. Because finding Pru in the middle of the plan made everything different. Suddenly, having a new friend, a real friend, seemed better than the plan, and maybe even better than going through with it.

Every day at recess, Pru and I went off to the soccer nets and kicked the ball around, discussing how to get the lacrosse equipment we needed.

"I guess I could ask my parents," I said on Thursday, without much hope. Chasing down my mom and pulling the cell phone from her ear wouldn't be easy. And lately, Dad looked too tired to talk. Besides, they might think lacrosse was too expensive. It was hard to tell. "I don't know, though."

Then I thought about Maxine's new makeup and shoes for the play and all the extra money Mom and Dad gave her for special dresses and gas for the car. "But they're always buying stuff for my sister," I said. "Maybe it's time they give me money for something I want to do."

"Maybe." She gave a Pru-nod and kicked the soccer ball my way. "It's worth a try." Pru ran ahead, and I passed the ball to her. "So, you ask your parents, and I'll ask Marty if there's any old, leftover equipment that the university coach might let us borrow. You never know." She took a wheeze-breath. "We might be able to get enough to start a real game after spring break."

The good feelings I had during recess disappeared as soon as Pru and I got back to our lockers. Sadie followed us, and the TCs moved like a shadow behind her. I took it as a bad sign.

"Jamie," she said, in a sing-song voice that sounded too friendly. I turned around to see her give a smirk at Pru. "You haven't played Tower Tag with us all week." She reached in her pocket and pulled out a tube of lip gloss. "I thought up a new position, and I wanted you to be it. But you never hang with us at recess anymore." She dabbed the gloss on her lips.

Sadie played that game a lot—ignore a girl, then act like friends again. Back and forth like friends were ping-pong balls. Sadie's nickname should've been Saran Wrap—that clear plastic stuff you use to cover leftover food. You could see right through her. Sadie didn't want me in the TCs, and I was an outsider now. But I'd found a new friend, and I don't think Sadie could stand that.

She waited for me to say something, but I didn't. My whole body froze. Sadie could do that to me. She had the power, and I'd pretty much given her all of mine. Her eyes tried to figure out how to melt me. "I'm sorry I didn't let you sit with us at Book Time the other day," she said. "But, you know. I've missed you at recess. I was just mad."

I guess her fake apology finally helped me speak. "That's okay," I said, even though it wasn't. My voice was wispy thin. "Pru and I just felt like playing soccer."

"Soccer, huh?" She didn't give a fake smile with her fake apology. "Well, don't ya need a team to do that?" She had eyes the exact color of the worms my dad and I used to fish for bluegill at the pond. And today, they seemed like bait. I could feel her waiting for me to bite on the hook.

"Pru—uh—Pru and I've been kicking the ball around. It's been fun." I tried to make my voice easy-breezy like hers, hoping she'd lose interest in me.

She turned then to include Pru in the conversation. "Since when are you friends with Pru Wheeler?"

Two things about her question made me super mad. One, she said 'Pru Wheeler' like a dirty name—a total put-down. Two, she didn't have a right to question my choice in friends. The girls stared at me, waiting, too.

I knew I had to answer. But deciding what to say felt like being on the balance beam in gym class and trying not to fall off. I didn't have much room to walk without slipping. I wanted the right words—to shut Sadie up without pushing her red-alert button. And I sure didn't want to stir up the Sadie wanna-bees. But when did the right words ever come when you needed them to?

Finally I answered, my voice weak. "I guess that's my business." I tried to stay level. Even. But my heart fell off the beam with a thud.

"What did you say?" Sadie took a step forward.

I think Pru understood how hard I tried to balance on that beam. We looked at each other for a second, and then she gave me a short Pru-nod before turning her eyes on Sadie. "I think if Jamie wanted your opinion about who she's friends with, she would ask you."

All the girls pulled back, like a dragon had just blown fire in their faces. And I wanted to laugh at how they stared at Pru, their eyes huge. But I stood terrified. No one *ever* talked to Sadie that way. Never. Like Pru had flicked a bug off her arm. And the words hung there between them, like a big fat dare.

"Really, hmmmm…." Sadie bit her bottom lip, trying to keep the surprise from her face. I moved a little closer to Pru, both of us stiff like statues. Sadie's eyes got hard then. They were kind of crazy looking, and she turned to the TCs with a smirk.

"Well, we'll leave you and Pru—" she gave Pru a once over, up and down with her eyes, "—*alone*."

I thought maybe that was it. It hadn't been so bad,

really. I'd expected worse. But as Sadie headed for class, she turned back, and all the TCs stopped to stand around her. "You *both* have Loser Syndrome." She smirked again. "L.S."

"Yeah, L.S.," the girls said together. And I knew as they walked off, whispering, all of them looking over their shoulders at me, that this wasn't the end of it. Sadie would make sure of that.

Lori J. Sawicki

Chapter 9
$100 to Go

When school let out for spring break, I could finally breathe. It felt great to leave the TCs behind for a week because being ignored by everyone, especially Sue Ann, was awful. I thought about my Aunt Judy's cake a lot, more than I ever had in my life.

But during that week, I spent every day with Pru, hanging out like real girlfriends, and that awful feeling almost disappeared. In the mornings, we practiced lacrosse on our own, and then Marty stopped by around dinnertime. After only a few sessions, I'd become pretty good at attacking, and Pru could defend like a pro.

In the afternoons, Pru and I rode our bikes into town to the animal clinic. She volunteered there, feeding the animals that had to stay overnight. The vets let Pru hold the dogs and cats getting shots or medicine.

Boy, those animals loved Pru! They'd curl up in her arms—even the ones that seemed extra scared. They calmed right down when she touched them, and I think they felt safe with her. She talked low, petting them in a real gentle way. Maybe those animals thought they had their mothers back, snuggled in close like that.

I asked Pru one day why she worked at the clinic. I mean, it didn't seem like what normal sixth graders did in their spare time.

"Because of my mom," Pru answered. "She volunteered there, and I went with her sometimes. She loved animals. After she died, the people at the clinic said I could come by any time." Pru sucked on her inhaler. "My mom always said you should spend just a little bit of time doing something more than worrying about yourself."

In between my time with Pru, I tried to build up courage to ask my parents for the lacrosse money. I'm not sure why I felt afraid. I mean, they were my parents, not Sadie. But I waited, until Pru finally pointed out that I couldn't expect courage to just walk up and be friends with me—not if I kept pushing it away. And even if I didn't have much, I only needed a little, like when I'd helped look for her contact lens.

That really got me—Pru thinking I had courage. I never felt brave that day; I just thought we should help. But Pru always saw something else in people. Something more. Especially in me. So, on Thursday of spring break, Pru got permission to spend the night, and I planned to ask for the money after dinner.

Marty dropped Pru off around 5:30, and my parents came home early from work. I think Mom wanted to make a good impression, to show we had a normal family, all eating dinner together at night—when really, Mom usually picked up fast food and brought it home. I don't think she meant to be fake or anything; she just wanted to act like a 'regular mom.' Maxine said once she thought Mom felt 'conflicted' about what that meant because she had such a busy job.

But instead, Pru came over and experienced Corman Zoo Night. You could smell food burning in the oven—a chicken and broccoli casserole that Mom had never cooked before—while Mom worked out another problem on the phone with Mike. Maxine yelled from upstairs that she needed me to find her cell phone because I'd been the last person to see her use it. Dad hollered that he'd managed to pop open the Pillsbury flaky biscuits, but he couldn't get them out of the container.

"Jamie!" Maxine yelled again, as Pru stood in the foyer with an overnight bag and pillow in her arms. I took them from her and put them in the living room. "Did you find my cell phone!?"

"No," I answered, much more quietly than my sister. "Why don't you use the regular phone."

I hung Pru's jacket in the closet and could hear Maxine sigh all the way downstairs—that's how loud it was. "Okay. Will you bring me the extension?!"

Pru gave me a raised eyebrow, and I rolled my eyes. "Want to meet my sister?"

"Sure," she said with a Pru nod.

I grabbed the phone, and Pru and I started to go

upstairs, when my mom came hurrying from the kitchen. She had her cell phone pressed to her ear and carried a pitcher of lemonade to the dining room table—a table we never used but had been set in Pru's honor.

"Oh Jamie, Pru's here!" she said, like I didn't know. "Hello Pru. I'll have to call you back, Mike," she said into the phone. "We have company." But she vanished back to the kitchen and kept talking.

"Come on." I motioned to Pru to follow me upstairs.

We found Maxine pacing around her room with a pair of purple tights in her hand. A heap of clothes covered the bed. Dresses hung on the closet doors and over the desk chair. And some kind of tornado had thrown every shoe from the closet into her room. A mound of curlers filled Maxine's hair—you know, those really big ones that stand up so high they look like they might snap your neck off if you tip your head too far in the wrong direction.

"Oh thank god!" she said when we came into the room. She grabbed the phone from my hand like a starving person reaching for a sandwich. I felt embarrassed that Pru's first meeting with my sister had to be during a night of Corman insanity, but I'm not sure when it would've ever been different.

Maxine punched the buttons on the phone, hopping

around on one foot, trying to put a leg into the tights. She nearly tripped and grabbed onto me for support. I hopped her over to a small clearing on the bed.

"She's in *Romeo and Juliet*," I said to Pru, detangling myself from my sister. "She's Juliet."

"Oh I love that play!"

Maxine glanced up then and seemed to see Pru for the first time. "Hi," she said, as she pulled on the tights. "You must be Pru." Maxine left a message for Ellen to call on our regular phone and then punched OFF with a groan-sigh. She tossed the extension into the pile of clothes that started sliding to the floor.

Pru nodded. "Hi."

Just then, the phone rang, and Maxine leaned into the heap of dresses to answer it. "Oh Ellen. Where have you been?! I've got dress rehearsal in two hours, and I can't find my cell phone anywhere!"

I motioned to Pru, and we left Maxine's room. I couldn't understand why she'd need her cell phone to rehearse the play, but I don't think Maxine ever felt completely dressed without that phone glued to her ear.

Dad called us to dinner then, and Pru and I went downstairs. Mom carried the very burned casserole into the dining room, but it slipped from her oven mitts and dropped onto the table with a loud thud. It missed the hot pads by a mile. The serving spoon flung out of the Pyrex dish and fell to the carpet. "Oh!" she said, looking around in surprise. Dad shouted from the kitchen that the rolls had browned up nicely, when crash! It sounded like a lot of dishes had smashed to the floor. Soon after, Dad shouted that there wouldn't be rolls or salad for dinner.

I walked over and picked up the spoon. Then, without my mom really noticing, I took the oven mitts from her hands and moved the casserole dish, placing it on the hot pads so it wouldn't burn the tabletop. After getting some wet paper towel from the kitchen, I cleaned up the chunks of chicken and broccoli spattered on the carpet.

When Maxine came down, wearing a robe and still the big curlers, she looked in horror at the casserole. "That's it?" she said, sitting down and then standing back up again. "That's what we're having for dinner?"

"Maxine, please." Mom flashed an embarrassed smile all around. "Welcome to our home, Pru."

****

We ended up ordering pizza, and Mom brought it to the table still wearing her black 'power suit'—a skirt and jacket she wore to important business meetings. She'd taken off her heels and put on slippers, but it still seemed to take her a while to remember she wasn't at the office.

"So Pru." Her voice had the business tone she always used on her cell phone. "It's nice to finally meet you How's school I'm happy you could stay over Have you lived in Wheatland your whole life Where do your parents work...?" She barely took a breath. I'm not sure she realized she'd asked three questions in one sentence.

"*Mom*. Gloria," Maxine and my dad said at the same time. They had the exact will-you-chill look on their faces.

"We usually do better than this," Dad said to Pru, interrupting Mom's attempt at conversation. "Most nights, we have our personal chefs at KFC and Wendy's cook dinner. But they were busy." Pru laughed out loud then went into a coughing fit.

When dinner ended, I sat at the table building up courage to ask my parents about the lacrosse equipment. I wanted to keep the whole conversation short because I knew Mom's cell phone could ring at any minute, and Dad looked ready to fall asleep.

Finally, I just blurted it out. "I need some money." The words were barely a squeak—my voice nervous, like when I talked to Sadie. I stabbed at a leftover piece of pizza crust with my fork.

"Okay. For what?" My dad ran his hands over his

face in a scrubbing motion.

I gave Pru a look, and she gave me a nod. "Um, for some lacrosse equipment."

"Lacrosse?" My mom barely got the question out before her cell phone rang. She started talking to somebody named Dee and disappeared into the living room.

"Sounds interesting," my dad said. "Is the equipment for you and Pru?"

"Yeah, and a whole lot more kids. We want to start up a team in our class."

"That's kind of exciting." He pushed back from the table. "I don't see why not. How much do you need?" He reached for his wallet.

He had a weary face, like maybe he wished he had time to learn lacrosse, too—time for anything besides his work. It was a look of going too fast and wanting to slow down. A sad expression, behind the tired.

Pru and I had done the math. We needed about two hundred dollars to get the equipment, if we bought beginner gear. But I didn't have the courage to ask for that much.

"Well, we don't need everything at once. If we just

had equipment for, well, maybe six players, it would get us started." I thought that was good enough. I didn't need to ask for it all right then. "We can use the soccer nets at school for now."

Dad pulled out his wallet and handed me a wad of twenty dollar bills. "Here's a hundred. That should help launch your new venture."

I took the money and smiled at Pru. It wasn't near enough but more than I expected.

Both Pru and I thanked him, and Dad tried to smile. "You girls have fun now." And he walked into the kitchen leaving Pru and me alone at the table.

"Okay," Pru said, eyeing the money in my hands. "We're on our way." She sounded chipper. Happy. "We just need a little more."

"Yeah," I said, shaking my head. "About a hundred more. And how in the world are we ever gonna get that?"

Lori J. Sawicki

Chapter 10
Snooping Isn't Always a Bad Thing

"We'll figure it out," Pru said, following me to my room. She sounded confident. Sure. "Maybe I can ask my dad, or Marty can help us. Let's just not worry right now. A hundred dollars is a lot to start with."

We sprawled out on my bed drinking Cokes and talking about our plan, when Pru said the funniest thing. "Your family seems nice."

I laughed, then choked on my soda. Pru leaned over and pounded me on the back. When I could breathe again, I said, "Mine?"

She gave me her Pru-nod. "Sure. Your mom tried to make a nice dinner for us, and your dad, well, he's obviously tired. But he's nice, too. He tried to joke around." She took a breath-wheeze. "Plus, he was interested in our idea for the lacrosse team. And he gave us all that money for the equipment. It was great of him to be so receptive."

I put my soda can on the nightstand and gave her the eyebrow. "You think *Maxine* is nice?"

Pru almost smiled. "Oh, she's not so bad. There's just a lot going on in her life. She's extra busy."

"Everybody in our house is busy."

Pru ignored my comment. "And you can tell how much she counts on you and loves you. She asks you for everything."

"Yeah. Like a servant."

"Oh, I don't know. Maybe more like a friend—somebody who definitely needs you."

I couldn't think of what to say, so I just shrugged. Pru saw things I didn't—even in people like Sadie and Maxine.

"Do you have some paper—a pencil, too?" Pru asked. "I think we should draw some diagrams for kids who won't know how to play lacrosse. Plus, write down the basic rules."

I pointed to my nightstand. "Maybe you and I should wear the same sweatshirt next week," I said. "You know, kind of like a uniform or something." I got up and walked into the closet to look for my Wheatland Elementary School sweatshirt. "And we still have to figure out where we're going to get the rest of the equipment money." I dug through a pile of sweaters on my closet shelf. "Do you have a Wheatland sweatshirt?"

When Pru didn't answer, I hollered out again. "Whatdoyathink? Should we wear our sweatshirts?" I finally found mine hanging next to my raincoat and pulled it from the pole, then I ducked my head around the side of the door. "Hey, do you have a Wheatland sweat—" But my voice froze, like I'd swallowed a popsicle. Pru had my poetry notebook open on the bed, and she was reading it. She looked up, her eyes kind of sparkling. Like a kid, when she gets a Christmas present. But her face tried to apologize.

"Oh, Jamie. I didn't know this was your special poetry notebook. Gosh, when I opened it, I just wanted an empty page. I tried not to read anything but—" She stopped. Her eyebrows pulled together like she wanted to explain. "I'd never snoop in your things. But I couldn't help myself. Your poem about the sun in the trees is just beautiful."

Now, I figured I had two choices. One, I could be mad that Pru got into my personal stuff—no other person in the world had ever seen my poetry notebook. Or, two, I could ask her opinion. There didn't seem to be much in between. Her eyes said she hadn't meant to snoop. And I think I believed that. Plus, she'd called one of my poems beautiful.

"Really?" I sat with her on the bed. "Which one?"

Her eyes nearly glowed. "Oh, the one you titled 'Hide and Seek.' It's so visual."

Again, I wished for a dictionary. Because maybe I understood what it meant to visualize something, but I didn't understand what it meant about my poem. "What do you mean?"

"Oh gosh." She turned the page back and read it out loud.

"Hide and Seek

Sunlight
behind the leaves
in and through
moving
in little pinwheels
tiny stars
burst
then disappear
until the wind
shuffles the leaves
and yellow-white edges peek
then dance
into view
    Jamie C."

Pru smiled. "That's just amazing. I can see the sun in the trees. Your words made me *visualize* it. That's a hard thing to do." She paused. "Have you heard of Robert Frost?"

I nodded, then shrugged. "He's a poet, right?" I remembered the book Pru was reading at recess.

The Power of Two

"Yes!" She leaned closer to me. "And he wrote this incredible poem called 'Stopping by Woods on a Snowy Evening.' You can just see the woods and the snow coming down and someone standing there wanting to stay and look at it forever." She talked fast, a wheeze coming from her chest. "I just *love* that poem." She stopped again, staring at the open page in my spiral notebook. "'Hide and Seek' reminds me of that."

"How do you know so much about poetry?"

She Pru-answered. "My mom used to read it to me."

Now, wouldn't you think her mom would've been reading nursery rhymes or Dr. Seuss books or maybe *Goodnight Moon*? "Your mom read you Robert Frost—like, when you were little?" I asked in disbelief.

But instead of explaining it, she just smiled and gave a Pru-nod. "Yes."

I didn't ask if she'd understood Robert Frost back then because I could tell his poetry meant something to her now. I just liked how we'd connected in a new way, and it surprised me as much as Pru did. My poems mattered to her. And as far as I knew, nobody had ever been impressed with anything I'd done.

Pru fussed with a contact lens then, and I started to put my notebook away, when she asked, "Can I read some more?"

Pru just kept knocking on the door of my life, and I didn't know if I could let her in. My notebook had secrets and private stuff I didn't want anyone to know. But there was a lot to trust about Pru. I wanted to say yes.

"Okay," I said, finally. "But do you want to do that now? We should probably write out the lacrosse rules for Monday."

"Yes. If you don't mind."

And that's how I spent my first sleepover with Pru. She sat on my bed, turning page after page of my notebook. Sometimes she exclaimed right out loud, "This is one of my favorites!" or "Wow, that's really great." Maybe she just wanted to be extra nice, but I knew that Pru had become a real friend that day—not because she liked my poems, but because she understood how much I loved to write them.

I'd never told anyone about that. Because the TCs had rules, and you couldn't do anything Sadie considered stupid. So, after Ms. Woods read some Haiku to us during English, and Sadie declared it "idiotic and lame! because it didn't rhyme, so what kind of poetry could it really be?" well, I decided not to tell anyone what I did in my spare time, or that I wanted to be a writer someday.

But it was so easy to share my biggest Jamie-secret with Pru. And later, after the worst thing in the history of sixth grade happened, I knew I'd never tell anyone again. Because no one would ever understand like Pru. Who would read each word, each line, and be so positive I'd become a poet? Who, except for Pru, would ever believe in the dreams of a middle-girl turned outcast?

Lori J. Sawicki

Chapter 11
Maxine's Three Ideas

In the end, Marty came to the rescue and helped solve our problem.

After taking us shopping over the weekend, he also called everyone on the U of M Lacrosse Team to see if they had old equipment we could borrow. By Sunday, we had a giant pile stacked up in the Wheeler garage: old sticks, helmets, used goggles, balls—enough stuff for two small teams. All the players wished us luck in our "new, exciting endeavor." I thanked Marty, and Pru hugged him hard.

Monday at recess, Pru and I dragged all the old and new equipment out to the soccer field. We propped the extra sticks up against the bench to show we had enough for lots of kids to play. The TCs tried hard to ignore us, but I saw them watching, especially Sadie, who looked out in our direction from the tower. I whispered this to Pru who gave me her Pru-nod. "It's going catch on. You wait and see."

But it didn't.

Pru and I marked off the soccer field and ran around playing a two-man game of lacrosse. I reached long with my stick to catch her passes. Pru ran ahead and caught mine. She could cradle the ball now like a pro. She moved close to the crease, about ready to shoot, but stumbled.

"Ball down!" I raced toward it, pretending to be Pru's opponent. Marty would've been proud at how I scooped the ball into the pocket of my stick.

We talked loud and laughed a lot—making it all seem really fun and that we knew what to do. We watched for anyone who might want to play, but no one did.

When I put away my jacket after recess, I could hear the whispers of the TCs at A-12. Their words moved in the air like dust, and I couldn't breathe. 'Stupid game,' 'sticks,' 'running around out there.' They giggled, and Sadie laughed louder than the rest. The locker door slammed, and they walked away. Someone said "loser." Someone else whispered "L.S."

It felt like drowning—swimming out too far from shore and everyone on the beach watching me go under. No one would save me. I swear, I tasted my Aunt Judy's cake like some kind of awful medicine. I wanted to run after them and say something to make things okay. But I couldn't. I'd turned in my middle status for a place on the bottom. It made me wonder if you could truly be a loser just for wanting to do something different at recess. For having a friend like Pru.

Instead of taking notes during history, I wrote a poem at the top of the page:

Loser Syndrome
What is losing? And who gets to say?
Are you a loser if you turn and walk away?
Can you stay strong to the one who's cool?
To the one who says that you're a fool?
Jamie C.

I didn't try to sit with the girls during Book Time now, and I ate lunch with Pru. I tried to accept being an outsider, hating to think the word in my head. I thought a lot about my new status. What did it mean if one girl went against the way things were? If she said "no," when everyone else kept saying yes?

Those questions bothered me a lot when lacrosse didn't catch on. By Friday afternoon, I came home gloomy, and pretty sure I'd traded in a boring but safe, middle-girl life for a lot of doubt and regret.

I sat at the kitchen table after school, trying to swallow down a Chips Ahoy! cookie with some milk, when Maxine hurried in. She dumped her backpack, flute case, varsity jacket, and track shoes on the table, flipping open her cell phone. "Hey Tweeter. Why so glum?" She punched in some numbers and pressed the phone to her ear.

I shrugged. Despite the milk, the cookie stuck in my throat, and I wanted to cry. I got up from the table and rinsed out my glass, so Maxine couldn't see my face.

"Tweets, what's up?" Maxine closed her cell phone with a sigh and opened the fridge. She seemed distracted, her voice uninterested. I waited until I knew I wouldn't burst into tears, and then I turned off the faucet and moved to stand in the doorway. It took a few more seconds before I could look at her.

"Nothing." But my voice asked for help. I wanted her to hear me.

Maxine pulled out bread, lunch meat, cheese slices, and mustard and sat down at the table to make what ended up being a very large sandwich. She worked fast, putting it together like she worked at a deli. "I know that face. What?"

I really wanted to talk to somebody. I'd ruined my life and knew I'd never have friends again—all because I wanted to do something different. So, I told Maxine, talking fast like she always did because I didn't want her to lose interest. I tried to sound braver than I felt.

By the end of my story, Maxine had chewed halfway through her sandwich in quick bites. I didn't think she'd been listening because she kept checking her cell phone for text messages. I figured our conversation gave her a way to kill some time. But after I stopped talking, she said three important things.

"Girls are always like that." She sighed.

"Like what?" I wanted to sit at the table with her,

but I stayed in the doorway. Maxine and I had never had a real talk, so I didn't trust it.

"Followers. And afraid." She said this like it should all make perfect sense.

I took a step back into the kitchen. "Afraid of what?"

My sister waved a hand in the air. "Afraid to be themselves. You guys always clump up in groups and move like schools of fish. Everyone's afraid to break out and swim upstream, you know, against the current. Like one fish has all the control, and everybody just follows along." She sounded a lot like Pru.

"Did you ever break away?" I couldn't see her being in the middle or being sent to the bottom. She'd always been the lead fish.

"A few times." She shrugged like it didn't matter. "Girls create a lot of drama. Once in a while, it's too much. You need to escape."

I didn't know what kind of drama she meant, but I knew that when someone's already cool, they're allowed to break away from cool because they'll always be let back in. My sister never had to worry about stuff like that. And, so, just as I thought Maxine couldn't help me, she said the second thing.

"But it sounds like despite all that, you found Pru. And that's pretty awesome, right?" Before I could answer, she said, "Having one real friend instead of a lot of people you just hang around with is, well, kind of great. Seems like when all the other girls deserted you, a better replacement came along."

I wanted to say that she couldn't really understand because she *had* lots of girls to hang around with. But I knew what she meant. And it helped me remember what I'd gained after my plan failed—and not what I'd lost.

Then Maxine came up with what seemed like a great solution to help make the lacrosse plan a success—the third thing. "And as far as lacrosse goes, the boys are the most likely to join in. So, if you want the boys to play, you have to think like a boy."

I wanted to say that Pru had five brothers, and so that probably made her an expert on the subject, but I didn't. Maxine had never taken this much time to talk to me, so I figured I should probably just listen. "Well, what are they thinking?" I asked instead.

"They like competition. A challenge. So, make it a contest."

"Whatdoyamean?" I walked over to the table and sat down.

"Make a poster or sign—that you're having tryouts.

Make it sound official." She waved the rest of her sandwich around while she talked. "It could say something like: Tryouts all week. We need the best! Wheatland Elementary School Lacrosse Team. Team shirts will be handed out on Wednesday. Something like that."

"But they wouldn't really be trying out. I mean, we want everybody to play."

Maxine got up and pulled a jug of milk from the fridge. "They don't have to know that." She poured some into a glass and sat back down. "The sign tells the boys a few important things: one, that you need excellent players, and that you're not looking for just anybody. That means a lot. Two, it's a new team, which makes it a challenge, and boys love that. Three, if you're handing out t-shirts, then it's serious. It must be a real team. Make it appeal to their *nature*, Tweets. I bet every boy in class will want to play."

I didn't know what kind of nature she meant or how you appealed to it, but it all sounded like something Pru and I could do. I wanted to ask Maxine another question, but her cell phone rang, and she stood up. "Good luck, Tweets," she said over her shoulder as she hurried out of the kitchen.

I called Pru and told her about my talk with Maxine. She liked my sister's ideas and said we should start work right away on a sign. She mentioned, in her Pru-way, how nice Maxine had been to be so supportive and offer such great suggestions. I didn't comment but said I'd bring over some design ideas for the t-shirts.

Later, leaning against the headboard of my bed, I thought about my conversation with Maxine. She had it right in a way, about Pru being a better replacement. I'd given up Tower Tag and the TCs and got Pru instead—a good trade, and I knew it. The hole left by my so-called friends didn't seem as big anymore. Because even with Pru being so tiny, she knew how to fill up empty space.

That night, I wrote another poem.

Surprise
Colorless days, no friends,
wondering
where they are, where they hide
why it's such a big deal to change
direction.
And then Pru
Like a surprise present
One purple iris in the garden
Standing taller than any other flower
Soft petals
Different
Unlike all the rest
Jamie C.

Chapter 12
Boys Join the Team

Pru and I spent practically the whole weekend working on the sign. On Monday, Mr. Wheeler drove us to school, and we lugged it from the car and put it in the hall until recess. Using a giant piece of board that Marty found in the Wheeler garage, we'd written on it with leftover paint from the basement. Ms. Woods smiled when she saw us bring it in.

At recess, we placed the sign by the bench where everyone could see it. And though I don't usually brag, I thought it looked pretty great.

Lacrosse Team Tryouts!

We need the Best!

Team T-shirts 4 ALL

Players!

Then Pru and I played lacrosse like we'd done every day the week before. This time, when kids walked by, they stopped to read the sign.

Something felt different that day—like when the weather vane at my grandma's house changed direction. And Maxine had it right: the boys seemed most interested. We could hear them talk—"What's lacrosse?" "They're starting a *team*." "They're gonna have t-shirts." On Tuesday, some of those boys sat on the bench and watched us. And something else happened, too: all the TCs stood in the tower, staring in our direction.

Then on Wednesday, everything changed for real. Just as I fed the ball to Pru, who closed in to shoot a goal, she turned her head and yelled, "Marty!" I turned, too, and saw him sitting on the bench with his friend Erick. "Jamie, it's Marty!"

We ran over to him, and he gave us both a high five. "You guys are looking pretty good out there." He grinned.

"What are you doing here? Hi Erick." Pru wheezed, out of breath, and Marty took her by the shoulders. "Slow down, Mouse."

She tried to relax, but couldn't. Finally, she took two puffs from her inhaler and seemed better after that. "What are you doing here?" she asked again. The look on her face was Marty-delight.

"Erick and I didn't have class today, so we stopped by to see how things were going. Ms. Woods said we could visit for a while. Has anyone shown interest in the game?"

I shrugged. "I think the sign's helped. But still, nobody's asked to play."

"Well," he said, slapping his knees with his hands as he stood up. "Let's see if we can't change that." And he and Erick took up sticks and went out onto our field. "You and Pru take that end. We'll see how well you stack up against the pros!"

We played against Erick and Marty for a few minutes before Matt, Aaron, and Jim—the fastest boys in class—came to stand by the bench. I saw them from the corner of my eye, and Marty saw them, too.

"Good pick-up, Jamie!" he yelled, louder than he had to. "Pru, that's some awesome cradling!" Erick joined in. "When are you guys gonna come play for Michigan!"

I knew that Marty could play harder, and he let Pru and me pass the ball when he could've easily intercepted. But the way he did it, Pru and I ended up looking pretty excellent. "You girls are hot!" he shouted when Pru fed me the ball, and I shot it in for a goal. Finally, he called the game, saying in a loud voice that we'd worn him out, and he needed a break.

When we sat down on the bench, the boys walked over. They kept staring at Marty and Erick's sweatshirts. "You guys play lacrosse for Michigan?"

Matt asked.

"Yeah." Marty held up his hand and fist-bumped him. Matt bumped back. "I'm Marty. This is Erick." He grinned and motioned toward Pru and me. "They've been training with us. They're starting the Wheatland Elementary School Lacrosse Team."

The boys glanced at each other, and then at us, like we'd become important, and I wanted to hug Marty. He never said Pru was his sister. He just made us sound cool and connected somehow with the university. I peeked over at Pru who tried not to smile.

"Can we try out?" Jim asked, finally. All three boys looked at Marty, and then at Pru and me, and then back to Marty.

"Well, you'll have to ask them. Erick and I are just here for training practice." Again, he didn't give us away—they could've been training with us, or us with them.

"Sure," I said, probably too fast, but I didn't want them to change their minds. "Do you know how to play lacrosse?"

The boys seemed embarrassed, but Matt tried to sound cool. "A little."

"Well, we can teach you what you don't know," Pru

said, her voice confident. "How about we practice some drills."

All three boys nodded, but you could tell they hoped Marty and Erick would stick around. We did, too. Because it felt weird to just start playing together like we were friends. So, Marty and Erick stayed for a while to help us get started. And by the end of recess, Matt, Aaron, and Jim had the hang of the game. They carried their sticks back to the school importantly.

"Thanks Marty. Thanks Erick," Pru and I said, walking into the building together. "Great practice." The boys followed a little behind us.

I hung up my jacket, and there was silence at A-12, the TCs huddled together waiting for direction from their leader. I knew they were watching me. It made me prickly all over.

But I didn't turn around. Instead, I pretended to have trouble with the equipment, and I called over to Pru. "Can you take some of the crosses, Pru? We have so many, they won't fit in my locker." I said it loud, trying to sound confident.

I don't know, maybe I felt bold. Because I wanted the TCs to know our plan was working, and that I'd survived. That I wasn't afraid to be an outsider—even though I still secretly wished for a way back in.

But that was never going to happen. You didn't

make changes, then have the world spin back into place. It didn't work that way—unless you were someone like Sadie, whose world spun just about any old way she wanted it to.

No, sometimes you had to be ready to stand by yourself. Or if you had some luck, you found a friend to stand with you. Most times, it wouldn't be easy. And sometimes, it would be scary. You'd be exactly like Aunt Judy's cake: left alone at the table.

Thursday night was Maxine's opening night in *Romeo and Juliet*, and I asked if Pru could come to the play with us. Mom and Dad said yes right away, though I'm not sure they actually heard me. It was Corman Zoo Night with everyone running around getting Maxine ready.

As usual, she couldn't find a thousand things she needed to take with her—most importantly, a pair of purple velvet hair ribbons that matched one of her costumes "perfectly!" She said this, almost hysterical, so Pru and I searched her room for them. I guess Pru had become her servant, too.

We sat in the school auditorium, waiting for the play to start, and Pru leaned over and asked, "Did you know that William Shakespeare wrote almost forty plays, including *Romeo and Juliet?*"

I shook my head. I didn't know much about William Shakespeare.

"He was a poet, too." She gave me a Pru-smile. "His plays *are* poetry."

"Let me guess. Your mom read you Shakespeare at night, too. Like, when you were four or something."

Pru's eyes got extra bright. "Oh yes. It was so beautiful to listen to, even though I didn't understand it then." She said it like she understood Shakespeare *now*, and I grinned. I'm sure she did.

"Like, listen to what Romeo says to Juliet," she went on. "Tell me this isn't poetry:

> O, she doth teach the torches to burn bright!
> It seems she hangs upon the cheek of night...
> ...Did my heart love till now? Forswear it, sight!
> For I ne'er saw true beauty till this night."

Pru wheezed as she talked. "Well, I left out some lines, but isn't that *amazing*? It's so beeeeauuuutiful." She leaned back with a sigh. "I'm really glad you invited me, Jamie. I just love *Romeo and Juliet*."

Okay, it sounded like gibberish to me. And how she could remember all those lines was a Pru-mystery. But I got how much she loved poetry and the memory of her mom reading it to her. Pru's face went all soft whenever she talked about her mom.

We sat there for over an hour, and the play totally confused me. All those weird 'anons' and 'come hithers.' Real people didn't talk like that, with sentences turned around so that a question or statement seemed backward, and I wanted to give up, until the final scene. That's when I started to get it. I couldn't take my eyes off the stage or my sister. The audience got quiet, like everyone was holding their breath.

When Romeo drank the poison and Juliet stabbed herself, I glanced over at Pru and saw she had tears in her eyes. And when the prince spoke the last words, Pru mouthed them right along with him, her hands clasped to her heart. She sniffed, and then people clapped like crazy.

My sister got a standing ovation, and after the play we took her to dinner. She was going to a cast party later, but Mom said we should celebrate as a family first. I was super glad Pru came with us because I didn't think I could take much more talk about a play I barely understood or watch my mom and dad act like my sister had become a Hollywood movie star.

But Maxine treated me extra nice that night, and Pru, too. She thanked us again for finding the hair ribbons and for coming to her opening night. A lot of people stopped by our table at the restaurant—students, parents, people from the play—and they all congratulated Maxine. Never once did she call me "Tweets."

It ended up being a great night, especially because Pru and I got to order anything we wanted off the menu, even the adult menu. So, we ordered giant cheeseburgers, chili fries—a plate bigger than Pru, I swear—and tall glasses of the restaurant's special kiwi lemonade. Because of Pru's allergies, she had to be careful that the fries weren't cooked in peanut oil. But the waitress said, no, they used vegetable oil.

I'd never had as much fun as I did that night. Having Pru with me made everything better, and even the grown-up conversation didn't bother me. I had a blast—the kind you know in your heart can't last, but you want it to. So, you soak it up, every single part, like the last few seconds of a rollercoaster ride. And I felt so good. Until Pru started coughing and wheezing.

At first it seemed like one of her usual attacks, and I waited for her to reach for her inhaler, but she began to cough much harder. It became more violent. She couldn't seem to stop. I reached over and pounded her on the back, not sure what to do, when suddenly she collapsed on the restaurant floor.

Dad practically launched himself across the table to Pru before I could move, and Mom called 911 on her cell phone. Plates crashed to the floor, glasses shattered, French fries flew—chili and cheese splattered Pru's clothes. My heart tumbled around in my chest.

I dropped to my knees and bent over Pru, her face whiter than the tablecloth just above her head. I pulled the inhaler from her pocket and put it in her hand, but she didn't respond. So, I put it between her lips and pushed. When she didn't move, I tried again and then once more—she usually took two puffs, but I gave her three. She looked like she needed it.

I think I screamed for help. The words echoed in

my ears from somewhere far off, the voice not mine. And then someone took hold of me under the arms and pulled me away as Pru's face turned even paler, her eyes glassy. People shouted. People swarmed around her, bent over her where I'd been. Someone pumped on her chest and breathed into her mouth like a kiss. I turned and buried my head into Maxine's dress. I couldn't watch.

I had a horrible feeling that Pru might die—that this would be the end of our friendship, and I hadn't known her long enough! The thought made me want to throw up right then. I didn't know much about death, but the idea that I might never see Pru again made me feel the forever-ness of it like a dark sky or the ocean at night.

Finally, somebody said, "She's breathing! She's breathing!" Then I heard a siren. My body felt broken like cracker crumbs at the bottom of the box. And that's all I remember. Soon after, men with a stretcher came hurrying into the restaurant, and they took Pru away, leaving me there, without my friend—my best friend—wondering what would happen to her.

Lori J. Sawicki

Chapter 14
Three Big Things

By the time we got to the hospital, Mr. Wheeler was already there, and then Marty came with the rest of Pru's brothers. My parents talked with Mr. Wheeler in quiet voices. Though his face stayed calm, Mr. Wheeler's eyes looked crazy scared. The boys asked a lot of questions, and Marty shushed them so he could listen in. Never once did Maxine make a call on her cell phone. She sat next to me, sometimes putting her hand on my arm.

When the doctor came to the waiting room and asked for Mr. Wheeler, we all got up and stood beside him. The doctor said he believed a food allergy had caused Pru to have an anaphylactic reaction—a term I'd never heard before. He asked what Pru had eaten at dinner, and when my dad went over our food order, the doctor nodded, saying the kiwi lemonade was the 'probable culprit'—kiwi being 'a relatively new allergen.' He assured Mr. Wheeler that Pru would be okay, and I didn't listen to much more.

Standing next to Mr. Wheeler, I felt his body relax a little. I think he'd been holding himself tight and had finally taken a breath. After that, I heard voices but didn't hear words. I just wanted to see Pru—nothing else mattered. And as Mr. Wheeler walked away with the doctor, I ran behind him, asking to come.

My parents tried to hold me back, taking my arms

and saying I could go in later. But I squirmed away and looked straightaway at Mr. Wheeler. "Please?" I asked again, tears in my eyes. "Let me see Pru."

I wanted to say that I *needed* to see Pru—that if I didn't see her right now, I would burst open. And I think Mr. Wheeler understood because he put his arm around me and said, "Come on," and I got to go with him and Marty.

Pru was sleeping when we got to her room, but she was breathing and not as white as the tablecloth anymore. Just seeing her made me feel better, and I felt like I could breathe, knowing she wasn't going to die.

That night, I wrote a poem in my notebook:

Almost Lost

Almost lost
A pale ghost
Fading away.
"Don't go"
I wanted to say,
Holding onto you, us,
With words, any words,
To bring you back.
If I could have
I would have

Said how much
You mean to me
Never to let you leave.
                    Jamie C.

****

Pru spent Thursday night alone in the hospital, and Friday I played lacrosse with the boys by myself. School felt empty without her, and I was glad for the weekend—not just because I missed Pru, but because Sadie made me the target of her red-alert. She pointed nasty words my way and shot them dead on.

"Hey Jamie," Sadie hollered to me that morning from A-12. "Where's your new lacrosse partner?"

I opened my locker and ignored her.

"Is she tired of you already?" I heard a snicker. "She better come back soon. Losers need to stick together! Sticks—get it?" The TCs burst out laughing.

When the last bell rang, I couldn't get away from school fast enough. I practically ran to Pru's house. The nasty comments from the TCs followed me like witches on Halloween—black shadows, darker than night.

I sprinted up the Wheeler front porch and knocked on the door, out of breath. When Dane let me in, I took the stairs two at a time to the second floor.

Boy, it was great to see Pru! She sat propped up in bed with the Scrabble board spread out on her quilt. I think she'd been waiting for me. I came in and gave her a hug, then we sat together for a long time playing the game without talking.

Finally, after I'd put down letters for 'relief' and scored eighteen points using a double word square, I said, "Were you scared?"

"A little," Pru wheezed. "But mostly because I know all the stuff I'm allergic to, and peanuts are the only food. It's always alarming to find out there are new things—like kiwi." Pru laid down all seven tiles, spelling 'startle' using my 'e.' She got 50 bonus points for using all her letters in one turn.

"I thought you were going to die."

My words sounded loud. Big. They bounced around the walls, and it took a while for them to calm down—sort of like the sound in the halls at school, just after the first bell rings. Pru glanced up and smiled, taking seven new tiles. "I'm okay, Jamie."

I wanted to believe it. I had to. Because the idea that she might not be was too horrible to think about.

****

The Power of Two

Pru came to school Monday like she'd never had an attack of anything, and we walked out onto our lacrosse field at recess with Matt, Aaron, and Jim. "We can carry the crosses," Aaron said, taking them from us with a lot of enthusiasm.

We divided into two teams—Pru and me, and the boys. It seemed easier than making a big deal of picking sides and then worrying about an extra man. Pru decided we should all play the middie position; that way, everybody could run around and cover the whole field. And Marty had told us to use a man-to-man defense, which worked okay, even though we were a person short. Pru and I gave the boys the advantage because they didn't know the game. We just hustled more and split ourselves between the three of them. Nobody played goal.

"Over here!" Matt yelled, his stick in the air. Jim passed the ball to him, but it went wide, and Pru caught the pass behind him. I ran toward our goal and out to the side. "Pru! This way!" But she dropped the ball, and Aaron made a good pick-up, passing it to Matt.

Running after Matt was hopeless. He moved too fast, so I went after Jim who played closer to me. When Aaron passed the ball to him, he missed, and I scooped it up. Slowing down as I got close to the crease, I passed the ball to Pru. Aaron made a good defender, but Pru did a quick cut back and swung around, making a side-arm shot into the net.

"Awesome shot!" Aaron said, giving Pru a high five. He didn't seem to mind at all that she'd scored. Everyone grinned.

We went to midfield for another face-off, and I floated over the ground, barely touching. I criss-crossed and cut sideways, and my steps felt less clumsy. I held the stick in my hand and became someone else. Different than I'd been before. It felt like dancing.

For sure, Matt, Jim, and Aaron brought us a lot of attention. Kids stopped and watched. Some pointed as we moved around the field playing a real game. And when we put the equipment away after recess, the TCs stared at us, amazed probably that boys stood at my locker, and then at Pru's.

On Tuesday, Ms. Woods did a great thing. She asked Pru and me to give the class a report on lacrosse as a sport. "Nothing formal," she said. "Just some general information—the rules, how it's played, and some history. We'll use it as part of our social studies curriculum."

So that night, Pru and I worked on our report, doing research on the internet and calling Marty at college to ask a few questions. He said he was proud that 'we'd put lacrosse on the elementary school map' and loved that we stood in the middle of it all. For the first time, being in the middle felt like something good.

After we gave our report on Wednesday, three big

things happened: One, more boys asked if they could try out for the team. Two, Sadie and the TCs came over to watch. For the first time in, well, *years*, they didn't play Tower Tag. Instead, Sadie sat on the bench, and the girls crowded around her. I saw them from the corner of my eye each time I ran past that side of the field. But I never looked at Sadie straight-on. I didn't want her to think I cared that she'd shown up.

And then on Thursday, the third thing happened.

Lori J. Sawicki

Chapter 15
When the Fish Follow You Upstream

After recess, Sadie followed Pru and me to my locker. All the TCs came, too. Sadie's eyes moved from me, to Pru, and back to me.

I decided I wouldn't speak first, and she made me too nervous to talk anyway. Instead, I waited, like having the entire TCs at my locker happened every day—a normal Jamie-event.

"So Jamie, yeah. Lacrosse is pretty cool. That's a cool game." She nodded her head, and the rest of the girls nodded, too.

"Well, Pru and I think it's fun."

I waited some more, moving just a little closer to Pru.

"Well, we were wondering if we can try out."

I knew this test. Her brown, wormy eyes expected us to say no. She *wanted* us to say no. And if we did, she'd be able to tell Ms. Woods that we'd been unfair and get us in trouble. I'd seen her do it before. Whenever Sadie didn't get her way, she twisted the truth all up in a knot and made some other kid seem guilty. Then, she could take over and be in control. I knew she wanted a confrontation—one where we'd look bad. But we surprised her.

"Sure," I said.

"Of course," Pru answered. "Anyone who wants to try out is welcome."

The girls stood in a hush. Then Sadie said, "Okay. Thanks." And they all heaved out a giant gasp of group air.

I waited until the TCs followed Sadie into class, then I turned to Pru. She looked at me with a smile, and I smiled back. Our plan had worked!

"Wow." I mouthed the word to Pru.

Pru gave a nod. "Good job."

"I don't believe it," I whispered, hanging my jacket on the locker hook.

"I knew they'd play," Pru said with confidence. "Once the guys started playing."

But I hadn't been so sure. Because girls in the middle didn't make change or move things in a new direction—and an outcast had no power at all. I felt a little shocked.

I shook my head. "I thought Sadie might try to

wreck the whole thing."

"I thought she might try to sabotage the game, too," Pru agreed, using a word that I didn't really need to look up. I got the idea.

Then, Pru gave me a rare grin. "I bet those girls are loving you about now—thrilled not to play that silly Tower Tag anymore."

I clapped a hand over my mouth to keep from laughing out loud.

But as I closed my locker, I had another thought—one that made my heart stumble a little. "So now what?" I whispered. "Do you think they'll just join in? And play like everybody else?" Suddenly, my good feelings were tainted with suspicion. Even with the happiness I felt, I knew there could always be problems with Sadie involved.

And Pru seemed to understand. "Maybe at first. Because they won't know what they're doing. Later though…," she lowered her voice, "…it's hard to tell what they'll do."

I wanted not to worry about it. Because the plan had worked, and maybe it would be the start of something better. A way for us all not to be lemmings. If Pru was right, maybe the TCs were tired of following, too. I guess it was possible. So, I decided not to stress over it. The TCs were trading Tower Tag for lacrosse, and that was amazing. And feeling a little awesome right then, I held up my hand to high-five Pru. She Pru-nodded and high-fived me back.

Chapter 16
Problems Solved

By Friday, we had two problems: One, we would need more equipment. Two, we needed a new way to deal with all the kids who wanted to play. So, Pru and I worked on the last problem first. We asked Ms. Woods for a box, and we put yellow and green pieces of paper inside with the names of each lacrosse position. Kids who wanted to play picked a slip of paper and took that position for the day. There was no 'commander'—just two teams: yellow and green—and Ms. Woods praised us for using such a 'democratic approach.'

That night, after dinner, I tackled the first problem: I asked my parents for more money.

"A lot of kids are joining our lacrosse team," I said to my mom and dad, who had a speed-eating contest going with their Kraft macaroni and cheese—Mom's version of a homemade meal for all of us. She still wore her red, I'm-running-the-show jacket for meetings with difficult clients. "But we need more equipment. And Pru and I think we should have t-shirts for the players."

Nobody answered. Mom checked her cell phone, and Dad stared at his food—the same way I'd looked into my bowl of Lucky Charms the morning after my plan failed. It never seemed like the right time to talk about anything.

"Did you guys hear what Jamie said?" Maxine

snapped her fingers in the air, and I looked at her, shocked. It always amazed me how she could just speak up like that, when she knew Mom and Dad had more important things going on.

"I'm sorry, Jamie." Mom put her cell phone on the table next to her plate and sighed. "I've been so pre-occupied. Things didn't go well at the office today. What were you saying?" Maxine gave me a go-on eyebrow.

"I—I was telling you about our new lacrosse team. It's going good. But we need more—"

Mom's cell phone rang. "Oh. Well, that's wonderful. Just a second, Honey. I really need to take this." She smiled and gave a raised finger that meant she'd be right back. But I knew she wouldn't. Mom moved to the living room like a tornado had whipped her from the table.

Dad woke up then. But only a little. "What were you saying, Jamie? You need a t-shirt?"

I twirled my fork around and around in my macaroni and cheese. I couldn't quite figure out how to get Dad's attention, but Maxine did it for me.

"*Dad.*" Maxine tapped her knuckles on the table. "Jamie needs money for extra lacrosse equipment and some t-shirts for her team. More kids want to play."

The Power of Two

I stared at Maxine.

My dad's eyes had glazed over like a Dunkin' donut, but he smiled and nodded. I think we could've asked him for money to buy beer, and he wouldn't have noticed.

"Well, it does seem like a viable project," Dad said, waking up a little more. His face had the same expression it did the first time I'd asked for the money—like he'd missed an important moment. He reached for his wallet.

"Here," he said, handing me another wad of twenties. "I probably should've given you more the first time." Sadness filled his eyes.

I looked at the money. Another hundred dollars. "Thanks, Dad," I said, and mouthed the words 'thank you' to Maxine before I left the table.

We ordered shirts from the Wear It Tomorrow T-Shirt Factory, and the next week, Pru and I brought more equipment, and t-shirts with the words WHEATLAND LAX printed on the front and back. The kids were in a frenzy to put them on, and when we got to the field, we looked like a real team.

After recess, I tried to collect the shirts, but no one wanted to take them off. The kids voted to wear them over their regular clothes for the rest of the day. Ms. Woods called the idea 'wonderful!' and said it showed 'class unity,' so Pru and I stood at the door before the final bell rang and collected them as people left for home.

For a few days, school seemed different to me—the yuck gone. I loved playing lacrosse with all the other kids. And even having the TCs with us every day didn't bother me. They didn't play very well and had a hard time keeping up. Mostly, they stayed somewhere in the middle of things, which seemed kind of funny.

Those days I stopped feeling like I was at the bottom, though I really didn't care that much anymore. And I forgot about being like Aunt Judy's cake. It felt like Pru and I rode a rollercoaster together, over and over, every day, and I never thought we'd ever have to get off.

Chapter 17
Pru's Mom

I spent all my spare time with Pru. We had sleepovers, lots of loud dinners with Pru's family, and hectic, fast-food meals with mine. We sometimes practiced lacrosse with Marty and his friends, and a few times Matt and Jim came by. Once in a while, I went with Pru to the animal clinic. And Pru asked to read every new poem I wrote. One day in early May, she said something I'll never forget.

"Jamie, this poem called 'Forever-ness.' Where did you come up with that?" She sat cross-legged on my bed, her eyes more serious than other times.

I shrugged. "I don't know. When you look at the sky, doesn't it seem like the black goes on, well, forever? The stars, too?"

"Sure." She chewed on the end of a pencil. "But to say, 'an ocean of stars, lit by the moon,'—oh my gosh. That's so *beautiful*. And so true." Pru got quiet, reading it again. Then, just as I pulled out the Scrabble board, she said, "You're an amazing, poet, Jamie."

I had a hard time believing it. I mean, come on, a poet? In sixth grade? "Thanks, but I think that's a little farfetched," I said, using a word I'd learned from Pru. "I don't think I'll ever be a real poet. My stuff bores Mom and Dad to death. And besides, it's just for fun." But I didn't mean it.

Pru put down the pencil and looked at me, her eyebrows all scrunched together. "You know I love your mom and dad, Jamie, but it doesn't matter at all if they're not interested in your poetry."

I stopped turning the Scrabble letters. It seemed a weird thing to say. "It doesn't?"

"No. Of course not." She plucked a contact out of her eye, held it up to the light, then popped it back in. "It only matters what you think about it."

I didn't know about that. I mean, could you really ignore how your parents felt? Didn't their reaction count?

"You can't let negative opinions dictate how you think. You can't take their lack of interest to heart."

I barely understood what she meant, but I got the part about not being interested. "Their yawning says a lot."

But Pru stayed serious. "Anyone who can create pictures with words the way you do, well, you're going to have a spectacular career." She stopped, then gave me a Pru-nod. "You'll do great things with your words, Jamie. I know you. You'll help people. You wait and see."

Pru said that a lot, about how I'd be a famous poet

someday. But sometimes, she seemed extra adamant about it—another word I'd learned from her. She always seemed so sure about me, in a way no one had ever been. And once in a while, it made me sure about me, too.

We talked a lot about poetry—how Pru loved to read it, and I loved to write it. She told me about poets I'd never heard of—especially someone named Emily Dickinson. So, I went to the library and checked out a book of her poetry along with Robert Frost's collection. But after reading some of Frost's poems, I told Pru his words sounded nice, but I didn't always understand them. She gave me a Pru-nod and told me I would eventually. To not give up.

When we weren't playing lacrosse, sometimes Pru and I hung out at the park. We both liked to fish, and we'd sit by the pond, throwing our lines in, talking. One day, a mother duck paddled across the water with six babies. The last two kept squirting out to the side in a wild zigzag, and it took a lot of quacking from the mom to get them back in line. "Renegades," Pru said with a laugh. "Like us." And without a dictionary, I knew exactly what she meant.

It was at the pond that Pru told me about her mom and how Mrs. Wheeler had died of an asthma attack when Pru was little. Pru said her dad never really got over it, though he acted much better now. She worried about him a lot and was glad when he started to show signs of life again.

I asked if she remembered much about her mom, and Pru gave me a rare Pru-smile. "Oh yes." She pointed at a bunch of trees near the entrance to the park. "She loved flowers, especially wild columbine—it grows over there near those oaks. We'd pick little bunches and put them all around our house. I used to come here with her sometimes." Pru looked out and across the water like she could see something on the other side that I couldn't. "We'd pick violets, too." She motioned to a row of pines. "There's a large patch of them by the woods."

Pru stuck out her hand, pointing at the ring I'd seen the day I helped look for her contact. A gold band set with a purple stone. "Mom gave me this a few weeks before she died. She said purple represented all the things she expected from her children: independence, responsibility, imagination, and self-confidence."

"She sounds cool." I think I would've liked Mrs. Wheeler a lot.

Pru nodded. "She wanted all her kids to be true to themselves. To be genuine. And to stand up."

I was pretty sure a dictionary wouldn't help me this time. "What does that really mean?"

"She wanted us to stand up for what we believed in. And to stand up for others." Pru paused, her smile filled up with memories. "Like once, she told me a story about a boy named Jimmy who lived next door to her growing up. The kids at school always picked on him because he had Down syndrome."

"What's that?" I asked.

"It's a condition some kids are born with. They have a special look that's different from other kids, and it sometimes takes them longer to learn things. Sometimes it's harder for them to speak and say what they mean."

"Kids were mean to him?"

Pru nodded. "Mom said they used to tease him. Call him names. Tell him he was stupid. Sometimes they'd steal his backpack from his locker."

"That's horrible," I said.

Pru nodded. "Mom thought so, too. She said it was repulsive and uncivilized."

Obviously, Mrs. Wheeler had a vocabulary just like Pru's. But I didn't ask for a definition. I had an idea about what she meant.

"What happened?"

"Every year, Mom and her parents threw a Halloween party for all the kids in the neighborhood. They turned the garage into a spooky haunted house;

they played games; and there were prizes for the best costumes. She said it was a lot of fun."

"It sounds great."

"Mom loved it. Until one year, some of the kids at the party told her she should stop inviting Jimmy. After calling him stupid and creepy, they said nobody liked him anymore because he acted too weird. They said it right in front of him."

"You mean Jimmy *heard* them?" A cold shiver crawled down my back.

"He heard all of it. And Mom said he started to cry."

I felt like I might cry. And it took me a second to shake off the image of Jimmy hearing *that* from people he thought were friends.

"What did your mom do?"

"She was really mad because they'd all grown up with Jimmy. He'd always been part of the group. So, she told those boys *they* were they only stupid, creepy people at her party, then she told them to go home. She said it really loud, so everyone heard it."

I couldn't imagine having the guts or the courage to do that. "Did they go?" I asked.

"At first, I guess the boys tried to brush it off saying they were just kidding. But Mom knew they weren't. And she couldn't stand that the kids in her neighborhood would be as mean to Jimmy as the kids at school. So, she made them leave."

"Wow. That's great," I said. "Amazing."

Pru's mouth gave a quiet smile. "Mom always did stuff like that. She used to say, 'Pru, you've got to take a stand in the world. And you've got to speak up when others can't or won't.' I didn't really understand it back then, but I kind of do now."

I looked at the trees branches, the color of lime green, ready to pop open in leaves any day. The air was melting with a promise of summer coming.

"You must miss her a lot." I didn't know if I should say it—something so private that might be hard to talk about. But in her Pru-way, she just gave me an honest answer.

"I do. I was really young when she died, and it was like having someone take away your favorite stuffed animal or the blanket you sleep with at night. I didn't feel safe for a long time." She wheezed then waited, pulling in a breath. "I always wondered where she went."

You know when someone asks the question *you* want to ask in class but you're too afraid? Right away, I felt relieved that Pru brought this up because I'd wondered the same thing when my grandma died. I didn't want the chance to go by without knowing what the smartest girl in the history of sixth grade had to say about it.

I cleared my throat. "Where—uh—where do you think she went? I mean your mom, after she died?" The answer mattered to me a lot.

"Dad said heaven, which I don't know about because it seems a little abstract." I had a hard time with that word, but I kept listening. "And Marty said to some place good. So, I always wanted to believe it was something like that. Somewhere in the middle, maybe. A little bit of both."

"Do you think there's a heaven—I mean, even if you think it's, well, whatever you called it?"

Pru blinked and looked up at the sky. "Abstract just means it's hard to understand. It's nothing that we can see or hold onto. But I guess I do. I mean, the sky is so big. Enormous. All that blue. And at night, all those stars. It seems like there must be something really good up there to be that color and create so many lights in the dark. Maybe a heaven."

"I bet she's some place good," I said.

She gave a Pru-nod then said something that surprised me.

"My mom would've liked you, Jamie. She would've liked your poetry, too." She turned to me. "And your family—your mom, especially."

I gave Pru a you're-crazy look. "My mom isn't anything like yours," I said. "Mine is busy. Really busy." I didn't know how to say what bothered me about that. "It's like, I know she loves me, but she doesn't have time. She has such an important job. And everyone at the office needs her. She's on her phone practically every minute."

"You're lucky, though," she said, shaking her head. "She's still here." Pru stopped, like she needed to decide how to say something not easy to say. "Even if your mom's distracted a lot, she's not a bad person. She doesn't mean to ignore you. It's just that—I don't think she knows you *need* her. Or want to talk to her. You don't really ask—for her help, I mean."

"I've tried," I said, not sure that was true.

"You should try harder. Make her listen. You're so good at everything, Jamie—you keep everything under control. It's hard to think you need anything. Or anybody."

I wanted to disagree with Pru. But honestly, I thought she might be right. I mean, I didn't interrupt my mom or pull the phone from her ear or tell her I needed to talk. I let her be interrupted and walk away.

"You should try to stop her. Just tell her what you want. Before—before it's too late. I'm sure she wants to know."

I didn't know if that was true either. The relationship with my mom seemed a lot different from the one Pru had with hers—more of a catch-me-if-you-can sort of deal. Mom ran around, doing something Maxine called 'multi-tasking,' and I watched her sometimes, wanting to grab her as she went past. I always tried to guess what the people needed from her when they called during dinner—like they hadn't just seen her for ten hours at the office!

We talked and talked that day, and I told Pru things I'd never admitted to anyone—about my family, and especially Maxine. About my fears that I'd always be in the middle. Invisible.

"When I'm around Maxine, I feel like some kind of weed, growing next to a tall sunflower," I said to Pru, pulling at the blades of grass near the base of the tree. "Like I'm in a shadow all the time."

"You talk like a true poet," Pru said. And that shut me up. Pru could always do that to me because she believed in me—in all that I wanted to be. I never quite knew how to answer her.

That night, Pru slept over, and she wrote a poem for me after I'd fallen asleep. But I didn't find it until weeks later. She'd written it on the last page of my spiral notebook—the greatest poem in the history of the world. And I cried forever after I found it. I cried a million tears that emptied me out and made me feel sure I'd never be happy again.

Lori J. Sawicki

Chapter 18
Nicknames

About a month before school let out, the huddle started.

Pru and I first saw it on Monday, right after Ms. Woods excused us for recess. The TCs came together like a football team—Sadie in the middle, squatted down, with all the girls gathered around her. They looked over their shoulders at us, someone would laugh, sometimes they pointed, and then they'd huddle up again.

Each huddle lasted less than a minute, but still, it worried me. And Pru admitted she was 'bothered by this new development.' The TCs had something planned…or wanted us to think so. And even though the lacrosse team was a success, I still felt nervous. When Sadie looked at us, her brown eyes were darker than dirt.

And right after the TCs started huddling, I noticed the changes. At first, it was small stuff—like Sadie making a fuss about picking the same position two days in a row. After pulling a 'defender' slip from the box on Tuesday and then again on Wednesday, she acted as if the world was ending. And maybe in a way, it was. *Her* recess world had definitely changed. Eventually, she traded slips of paper with one of the TCs, so she got to play goalie. After the game, I told Pru that Sadie was good at getting her own way. She agreed, saying she wasn't surprised at Sadie's ability to 'work around the rules.'

But on Thursday, I noticed bigger stuff. Sadie was playing dirty. Twice, she fell down and accused Pru of tripping her. And once she tripped Pru, grinning as she ran by. A few times, Sadie played in the wrong position. But when Pru called her out on it, Sadie made such a commotion denying it—saying we needed a referee or *someone* to resolve problems on the field— that Pru let it go. Sadie's plan was getting clearer.

By Friday, when Sadie threw down her stick and stopped the game, walking to center field with the lacrosse ball, I understood her plan completely. She was trying to take control.

"So, Jamie," she said, tossing the ball back and forth, catching it with one hand, then the other. All the kids came to stand around us. "I'm having trouble figuring out who's on which team. All the shirts are the same color, so I'm getting confused."

The TCs bobbed their heads in agreement, and I held back a big sigh. But before I could speak, Pru did.

"Maybe we can borrow some blue masking tape from Ms. Woods, and one team can put Xs on their shirts. That would be easy to do."

I could tell that Pru wanted to end the conversation fast, but Sadie didn't. She gave Pru a long, smug look and waited. I think she enjoyed all the attention focused on her.

"Well, that's not going to help us for *this* game, is it?" She took a step forward. The TCs nodded again. Most of the other kids didn't seem to care.

"I think everybody can figure it out," Pru said, looking around at all the kids. "How many people are on the green team?" she asked. A bunch of hands went up. "And how many are on the yellow team?" More hands went up. "See? I think everyone knows which team they're on."

Sadie looked at Pru, then at me, her dark eyes catching fire. And just when everyone was getting restless, she said, "But have you noticed how nobody really knows what to *do*. Everyone's just running around, playing positions, but the teams don't have a game plan. You know, like in football. Each team has a coach—a leader. Somebody to help them with tactics and a *strategy*."

I'd seen this before. Sadie would try to mess things up by pointing out something wrong—something that didn't matter at all. I'd watched her do it with Ms. Woods when she didn't like a new class project or her partner for a math game. She was good at coming up with ways to confuse people.

But I wasn't confused. I could see through her Saran Wrap. Sadie would get attention by making it seem like something was wrong—that the teams needed 'management' or leaders with playbooks and secret formations. And when everyone was mixed up enough, she'd go after what she wanted.

Just then, the bell rang. We all stood there, unsure of what to do. Sadie's words hung over the lacrosse field like a question mark, but we didn't have time to discuss it. Heading back to class, no one said much—like something was left undone or there were decisions to be made, but no one knew what they were or why we should make them.

Back at our lockers, I turned to see Sadie watching Pru and me. Her eyes were squinted into tiny slits, her smile more like a smirk. And even though I wanted to feel proud of our plan, and that we were all playing together without a leader, I knew Sadie wouldn't let this be over. Not until she had control of it all.

****

I wanted to talk to my sister about it, but chaos reigned at the Corman house. Maxine spent every night preparing for the Wheatland Miss Teen Pageant, and she had the spotlight. So, whenever Mom or Dad had an extra minute, Maxine got it. I decided I'd have to deal with the huddle issue on my own.

Friday after school, when Pru came to spend the night, the chaos was out of control. Maxine summoned me to her room. "Tweets! My zipper's stuck!" I knew that frantic I'm-trapped-in-my-dress call. Pru and I moved off my bed and wandered down the hall.

"Tweets, try to pull it down without ripping the material." Nearly out of breath, she hopped back and forth, rubbing the back of her neck with one hand and clutching her cell phone with the other.

"Hold still." I waited until she quit moving.

When I finally got Maxine unzipped, she hung the dress on the closet door. The long black material had a matching jacket with tiny purple flowers embroidered on the jacket sleeves. It got a Pru-smile. "That's a pretty dress. Is that for the pageant?" She wheezed her question like she had no air.

Maxine nodded. A couple of pink curlers flopped around dangerously on her head. "Uh huh. Do you like it?"

"A lot," she said. "If you win, do you get to wear a tiara? You know, a crown?"

"Yup."

"Jamie said you won the Wheatland Young Miss Pageant when you were twelve."

"I did." Maxine gave Pru a grin. "Why so

interested?"

Pru shrugged. "Oh no reason." She glanced around Maxine's room. "Did you win a crown in that pageant?"

Maxine pointed. "Yeah. It's over there in the drawer if you want to see it."

Pru went to the drawer right away and pulled out the rhinestone crown. She gasped, holding it up to the light, turning it around and around. Maxine smiled. "Go ahead and try it on if you want." She reached up and re-rolled one of the loose curlers. It amazed me that she could do it without a mirror.

Pru turned around so fast, I thought her mouse-neck might break. "Really? I mean, no that's okay." But I knew she wanted to.

"Go ahead," Maxine urged. "Jamie was never interested in that kind of thing. Thinks it's silly, don't you Tweets?"

I hated that she used my nickname in front of Pru, but Pru didn't seem to notice. She stared at the crown. "Well, if it's really okay…." Her voice faded out.

"Sure. It's fine."

Pru moved to stand in front of the mirror and put

the crown on her head. Pushing the little combs into her hair, she stood back, turning this way and that—acting all girly, which wasn't like Pru at all.

"It's beautiful," she said in her quiet Pru-way. "I bet you loved it."

Maxine nodded as she searched in the closet. "You can wear it if you want."

And Pru did. The rest of the night. She wore Maxine's tiara around the house, to dinner, and later while we ate popcorn and watched TV. She didn't seem embarrassed at all. And though it became a joke between us, I knew Pru loved that crown. Maybe when you lived in a house full of boys, it felt good to dress up. Or when you got a chance to trade a lot of guy talk for a girls' night, you made the most of it. I don't know. I'd become familiar with those Pru-contradictions.

Later, when we got in our pajamas and Pru finally gave up Maxine's crown, we lay in my double bed, mostly all talked out. But just as I was falling asleep, Pru asked, "Why Tweeter?"

"What?"

"Why does Maxine call you Tweeter?"

I yawned. "That's how I pronounced 'sister' when I was little. Maxine always thought it sounded cute."

I could feel Pru smile. "That's nice."

"Seems kind of stupid to me." I yawned again.

"No, it's special," she said, rolling over. "The way Marty calls me 'Mouse.'" And then, after a long pause, she added, "It means she loves you extra special."

Now, I'd never thought Maxine's nickname for me meant anything special, that's for sure. And I felt positive it didn't mean anything about how much she loved me. But the idea kept me awake for a while. Marty and Pru had a different kind of relationship—nothing like the one I had with Maxine. But Pru had a funny way of seeing things, clearer sometimes, and I wondered if what she said could be true.

When I closed my eyes that night, I didn't know it would be the last time Pru ever slept over at my house. If I had, I might've tried on Maxine's crown, stayed up late watching TV, or dragged Pru to the kitchen for extra cookies and milk. I might've done a lot of things a different way. But life's like that. You just never know. And you can always think about what you would've done, after the fact.

Chapter 19
When Everything Changed

By Memorial Day weekend, about three weeks before school let out, the Wheatland Elementary LAX Team was a success, sixth grade was almost over, and summer break waited for us like an ice-cold soda at the end of a long game. We couldn't wait to drink it! The TCs still huddled at every recess, but Pru and I ignored them now. I felt sure the yuck feeling was gone for good.

Over the holiday, the Wheelers had a barbeque with a lot of relatives. Mr. Wheeler said "of course" I could come, and so Pru and I spent the afternoon playing lacrosse with her cousins. I could feel summer coming, filled with tons of free time, long days with Pru, and lots and lots of sleepovers.

Food covered the picnic table in the backyard with nothing that looked like my Aunt Judy's cake. And just after I'd squirted some mustard on my hotdog and heaped a huge scoop of potato salad on my plate, my life changed. Forever. In that moment, the future came sooner than it should have, and the world became a different place.

It happened quick, like a flash of lightning at night through the window. I stood near the end of the picnic table, holding my plate, when I saw Pru get up so fast, she knocked over the lawn chair she was sitting in. Then she slapped at her neck, brushing at her ear.

"Dad!?!" Pru's eyes got big, looking for him across the yard. The plate of food slipped from her hands.

Time stretched out, at low speed. Pru stood there, waiting, holding her neck. She looked surprised, then scared, super afraid—in a way I'd never seen Pru before. She rubbed at a spot just below her ear, over and over. She seemed to move in slow motion—the way you see on TV, when everything almost stops, so you can see all the details.

Then she put her hand to her throat, coughing, wheezing, breathing hard, gasping for air, and everything sped up again. Pru's legs got wobbly, people started shouting, and Pru collapsed by her chair. Mr. Wheeler raced across the lawn. Marty knelt next to her. I threw my plate on the table and ran to her.

"John, call 911!" Mr. Wheeler yelled to his brother who was already punching numbers into his phone.

Marty searched the pockets of Pru's shorts for her inhaler and pumped some into her mouth. Mr. Wheeler yelled for more help. "Dan, get the epinephrine kit! It's under the kitchen sink!" Pru's Uncle Dan ran into the house, bringing it back right away.

Mr. Wheeler opened a box and took out a needle, stabbing Pru with a shot right in the thigh. It seemed like it would hurt a whole lot, but Pru didn't cry out.

"Come on!" he said, his voice low. After a few

seconds, he took out another needle and did it again. This wasn't like the night at the restaurant, and I knew it.

I moved on my hands and knees next to Marty who sort of sprawled over her, on his own hands and knees. Sirens whined in the distance and people screamed. And all the things I'd ever been afraid of before in my life, gave way to a bigger fear.

They say when people are scared, they turn white as a ghost. But white is still a color, I think. When the ambulance came, Marty's face changed to the color of nothing—of empty. He jumped into the ambulance with his dad, and he didn't look afraid. He looked blank. His eyes had no life as the doors slammed, and the ambulance drove away with Pru.

Right then, I knew what a heart attack was like. I could feel a crack about to split my heart in two. Huge pain ripped both sides apart. And I knew, as I watched the ambulance disappear down the street, Pru might die. Relatives cried, and neighbors hugged Pru's brothers. It all seemed so final—like the last scene of *Romeo and Juliet*. But I refused to believe it. I wouldn't. Pru's doctors would know what to do, the way they did after she drank the kiwi lemonade. And besides, who ever heard of somebody *dying* because they ate some peanuts or a slice of kiwi?

My stomach twisted inside out, and I felt sure I'd be sick right there in the Wheeler backyard. But I wanted to go to the hospital. And when I saw Pru's Uncle John and Aunt Margaret getting into their car, I ran to them on shaky legs asking for a ride. Neither of them argued or gave me any of those adult excuses like "you're too young," or "it's best if you stay here." Uncle John just nodded, and I hopped in the back.

When we got to the hospital, Uncle John screeched to a stop under the red EMERGENCY sign, and we all ran into the building. I hoped for good news, but the next few minutes changed a nice barbeque Saturday into the end of the world. Walking down a short hall, we turned the corner into a waiting area, and there sat Mr. Wheeler clinging to Marty, arms around each other, crying. And I knew the worst thing in the history of my life had happened.

Marty buried his head in his dad's shoulder, and the two of them sobbed. Sounds came from both of them— a moaning that made my stomach twist up tighter than before.

Pru's aunt and uncle went to them and knelt in front of their chairs, forming a little group together. Uncle John patted Mr. Wheeler on the back, and Aunt Margaret held Marty close. At that exact moment, I knew Pru was dead.

I sat down in a chair by the door filled with a loneliness so big it could've swallowed me. The emptiness was deep, and it came with a feeling of never-endingness—the same kind I'd written about in the poem Pru liked so much. Right then, I felt lost in the night sky, sinking into a billion stars, never to be found, understanding for the first time the bigness of the world, endless—the forever-ness of it.

It was a forever-ness that changed your life and took you under and never let you go. I started to shake all over, knowing the world was showing me the future before I wanted see it. A future without Pru. And I cried. Because she'd disappeared into a forever-ness that I couldn't share with her—one that, I knew, would never let her come home.

Lori J. Sawicki

Chapter 20
Marty

The morning of the funeral, I went to the park and sat by the pond after telling my parents I needed to be alone for a while. I knew if I had to hear them ask, "Are you okay?" one more time, I'd explode.

I looked out across the water, lost in a lot of emptiness. It moved beside me, around me...everywhere. I couldn't think about a life without Pru. No more Pru-wisdom or Pru-nods. The best part of my life ended at the Wheeler family picnic.

Pru died of anaphylactic shock—more words I didn't understand. Even after she was gone, I still needed a dictionary. She'd died from a bee sting! From a stupid little insect. Anger sliced me up into tiny pieces—into little Jamie slivers. Not whole.

I walked to the woods and saw the patch of violets growing outside the trees, just like Pru had said. I bent down and picked a big bouquet, the clouds making cold shadows on my back. I cried, gathering up the Pru-colored flowers. The color of everything good—the color of our friendship. I looked at the purple in my hands and couldn't stop crying. Finally, I put the bouquet down in the grass and stretched out beside it, burying my face in my arms. The yuck feeling came back in a wave that nearly drowned me.

I didn't understand about dying because I'd only

been to one funeral—my grandma's. I remembered that her casket had been put in the ground and covered with dirt. And it really bothered me that they'd put her beneath the grass, like she'd been planted underneath it. I refused to think of doing that to Pru. The thought of her being underground made me want to die, too.

I don't know how long I stayed like that—drowning in the forever-ness without Pru—but I finally pulled myself from the ground and sat up. When I did, I felt someone behind me. And for a crazy second, I thought it might be Pru. I turned around, squinting up into the sunlight. It was Marty.

"Can I sit down?" he said. When I nodded, he sat cross-legged next to me. "I stopped by your house." He spoke in a low, soft voice. "Your parents said you were here. I hope it's okay that I came."

I nodded again. I didn't think I could talk without crying.

Marty looked at the violets gathered in a bunch on the grass. "Those are pretty. Pru's favorite." His voice cracked. He could barely say the words. "Are you bringing them to the funeral?"

I took a deep breath, pushing the hair out of my face. "If that's okay."

"Pru would love them."

Marty's voice shook, his face extra tired. The laugh in his eyes, all that shine—gone. I could tell it'd taken a lot of energy for him to walk over to the park to find me. He seemed broken. I think he felt the endlessness, too.

"I wanted to tell you something," Marty continued, "because, well, today is going to be pretty busy, and I might not get a chance to talk to you later."

I looked over at him and waited. The split in my heart got bigger to see him so sad. He was trying hard not to cry...not to crumble. And I knew Pru would've wanted me to help Marty because she'd been his 'Mouse,' and he'd had an extra special love for her— with a deep forever-ness. But I also felt sure, more than I'd ever been in my life about anything, that no words from me would ever make him feel better.

Finally, when Marty could talk, he looked deep into the woods, then up at the trees. "I wanted to thank you for agreeing to speak at the funeral today." His voice sounded stronger now, like he'd released some awful pressure that let him go on. "I know it was a lot to ask. I mean, my god, you're only eleven." He shook his head, and I knew what he meant to say—that there shouldn't *be* funerals for eleven-year-olds, and that none of this should ever happen to kids our age.

"It's okay," I assured him.

"Well, I'm not sure that it is, really. Because an

eleven-year-old isn't supposed to give a eulogy at her friend's funeral." I'd never heard of a eulogy, but I figured it had something to do with the poems I'd promised to read. "But Dad and I are glad—and appreciative. Because we know how hard this is for you."

I felt tears coming again, and I gave them a push, hoping they'd move back and give me room to talk. No matter how hard it felt for me, my love for Pru could never match Marty's or Mr. Wheeler's, even if the hurt felt as big.

"I think it might be harder for you," I said, trying to sound mature. "But I want to do it."

It seemed like a small thing to read some poems for a friend, though it would never be enough. I wanted to do more, something big. To shine a light on all her Pru-ness. But I only had poetry to give. And because Pru liked mine so much, it was the best thing I had—a secret gift from me to her.

I felt Marty looking at me, and I turned to look at him. He had the saddest smile on his face. "You know, Pru was right about you."

"Right about what?"

Marty looked back at the trees. "Pru didn't have a lot of friends." He said this like maybe I didn't know. "She pretended it didn't matter that much to her—you know, that she managed okay by herself. But she always wanted a real friend. And after Mom died, well, she was really lonely."

I waited for him to finish. He rubbed the back of his neck like he'd slept wrong—though the circles under his eyes looked like he hadn't slept at all. Finally, he said, "Pru told me once that you were the best person she ever knew."

Marty made it sound like a fact. Just because Pru had said it. "She told me you always knew how to help people and that you knew exactly the right things to do." He paused, picking up one of the violets from the grass. He twirled it around and around between his fingers, and then he turned and handed it to me. "I think she was right."

We both got quiet, and I stared at the violet. All this time, I'd thought of Pru as the best thing in my life, and there she'd been thinking the same about me. What a surprise, really, because I'd never been the best thing in *anybody's* life. I took the flower and felt my heart break a little more.

Marty glanced at his watch, and as he did, I saw he had Pru's ring on his pinky finger. It barely fit over his knuckle, and I thought I might die then, my heart ripping open forever. "I guess we should get back."

I put the flower Marty gave me in the front pocket of my shirt and nodded, picking up the rest of them, holding them like they might break. Together, we stood, and with Marty's arm wrapped around my shoulder, we walked through the park, near the oaks, where I stopped to pick a handful of wild columbine. "Let's get these for your mom," I said, and Marty agreed with a smile, knowing exactly what I meant.

Chapter 21
Poems for Pru

Mr. Wheeler asked if I would sit with the family at the funeral, so I squeezed in the front pew next to Marty. My parents and sister sat behind me, and every once in a while, during the service, I felt one of their hands on my shoulder.

I tried to keep my eyes straight ahead, but it was hard not to look at Pru's casket. Flowers covered the little metal box, my bunch of violets and columbine mixed in with the others. It's really true about getting a lump in your throat when you're upset—mine felt like the size of a golf ball, and I couldn't swallow it down.

When the minister asked me to come to the podium, he said, "Pru's best friend Jamie Corman would like to say a few words." And I felt that lump grow to the size of a baseball. It all seemed so final. So over. I knew when I was done talking, Pru would be done, too. Maybe Marty understood because he took my hand and walked with me up the stairs. He stood just behind me where I couldn't see him, but I could feel him. I heard the minister's words, "best friend," "best friend," like Pru was beside me, whispering them in my ear.

I stood at the microphone but didn't feel scared. A lot of people had come for Pru's funeral—friends from the clinic, Marty's lacrosse buddies, Ms. Woods, and others I didn't know—and they all watched me, but I didn't really see them. Maybe when you're doing something for a friend, and you want to remember them the best way you can, being afraid isn't really an option. It would be selfish, anyway, to give in to fear, after you've lived through the scariest thing of all, and other people are more scared than you.

"I'm going to read two poems today," I said, trying to clear the baseball out of my throat. "Pru liked poetry a lot, and one of her favorite poets was Robert Frost. I don't know if you know him or not, but he wrote some great poems, and Pru taught me to like them, too. And she liked Emily Dickinson and Shakespeare. So, I wrote two poems for her—because I thought she might like that." I gave a quick look at Mr. Wheeler, who gave me a smile.

"The first poem is called 'Pru's Footprints.' And the reason I wrote this is because, well—" I started to choke up, and I had to push hard against a big, fat gush of tears, "—because it's about, sort of about not following the crowd because—because Pru never did." I stopped, remembering the talk we had, not sure if I wanted to cry or smile. "It's about not being a lemming." The people in the church laughed softly at this. "And I wrote it because Pru taught me about not being one—a lemming, I mean."

Suddenly, the poems didn't seem good enough—to say who Pru really *was*. To tell about all her Pru-ness. And even with Pru's belief in me, as a poet and in the 'spectacular career' she thought I'd have someday, I felt afraid to read them—because they'd never be as good as Robert Frost or Shakespeare.

But it's all I had. The only thing to offer Pru in these last minutes with her; the only way I knew how to say what she meant to me. With poems.

As I tried to figure out how to go on, I glanced out at my mom and dad, and Maxine, who sat with you-can-do-it expressions. Maxine mouthed something to me that I couldn't understand. Then I felt Marty's hand on my shoulder. He gave it a squeeze. He gave me courage. Enough to share my writing, for the first time, with a church full of people I barely knew. In two poems just for Pru. I started to read.

"Pru's Footprints

Pru's footprints were small,
but they left a lasting impression.
When she walked into your life,
you knew she was there.

If you spent time with her,
she took you in a different direction...
toward books
and famous poets
and purple flowers.
Her path went to new places
instead of where everyone else was going.

Pru walked on a road
that led away from the crowd.
She didn't walk with lemmings.
She didn't follow.
And she wasn't afraid to walk by herself.
Her footsteps were special,
the kind no other shoes could make.

When people walk on beaches
their footprints get washed away by the sea,
but Pru's will remain,
leaving forever marks in the sand.
Her prints were soft, but deep,
And they'll never disappear."

I looked out at the people. Some smiled. Heads
nodded. It made me think they understood the poem,
and how Pru had been different. Special. And that she'd
always walked on a path that no one else had ever been
on. I glanced at Maxine who gave me a teary-eyed
thumbs up.

"And that was Pru," I said. "She wasn't like
anybody else. I mean, how many kids read Robert Frost
in the sixth grade?" I heard more soft laughter. "Or
spend their free time with sick dogs and cats or could
come up with the idea to start a lacrosse team?" I
paused, catching my breath, which was about to leave
me. "So, I just have one more poem. And it's about our
friendship. And—and why she was my friend. Uh—my

best friend."

The words on the paper started to blur. And right
then, I missed Pru winking and blinking as she fixed
her contact lens, and her big vocabulary, and her short,
Pru-nod, and hanging out at the pond. I felt the forever-
ness grab me by the throat, and I didn't know how to
pull its fingers apart. But I knew I had to. For Pru.

"The poem is called 'Pru Sunshine,'" I said,
fighting tears.

"Light through my window
Pru was the sun,
Her sparkle was pure
Over everyone.

A soft, gentle shine
A smile full of warm
She could push back the clouds
Of a coming storm.

To a distant place
She's traveled now
And I must go on
Without her somehow
To find new light

A new place to begin
To find new friendship
All over again.

Beyond the sun,
She's with the night,
But I see her still
She still shines bright.

A tiny beacon
Way up high
She's a starlight now,
In my night sky."

When I finished reading, I took my papers and started away from the podium, and that's when I saw people crying. Some dabbed at their eyes with Kleenex, and others sobbed. Mr. Wheeler held one of his sons who leaned against him. I heard loud sniffing noises.

"Thank you, Jamie," the minister said, as Marty and I went back to our seats. "That was lovely." And when I sat down, Marty took my hand and held it during the rest of the service, which I can honestly say I don't remember much about because I felt pretty sure I'd died inside—lost in the stars. Never to be found.

Chapter 22
Saying Goodbye

The Wheelers had lunch at their house after the service. A lot of relatives from the Memorial Day picnic showed up, but nothing about it felt like a party. I answered the door each time the bell rang. It seemed like the thing to do. People handed me food, and I put it in the kitchen. When bowls emptied out, I filled them up and took them to the dining room table.

I checked on Mr. Wheeler and Marty every so often, making sure they at least had something to drink. I knew they didn't feel hungry, but I could pretty much get them to sip on a soda or an iced tea. A lot of Marty's lacrosse friends came, and some of them said hello to me, and I got them drinks, too. The veterinarians from the animal clinic talked to me and said if I ever wanted to come by, they'd love to see me.

One time during the lunch, I saw Mr. Wheeler rub his temples like he had a really bad headache. So, I went into the bathroom, found some aspirin, and brought him two. He looked at me, surprised, and then thanked me, swallowing them down.

When I felt sure no one saw me, I went upstairs to Pru's room and shut the door. Everything looked the same as the last time I'd been there. I sat down on her bed, staring at the violets on the wallpaper. I looked at the shelves filled with all her books. Pru's contact lens case and solution sat on her desk next to her inhaler.

New summer clothes hung over her desk chair—shorts and shirts that still had the tags on. And folders and library books sat in a pile on the floor along with her backpack in the corner. It seemed she was almost there. But right in the middle of everything—she wasn't. Gone. A whole person missing.

I got off the bed and went to the bookshelf, taking down *The Complete Works of Robert Frost*, holding it against my chest. I closed my eyes and saw Pru's face the first time she told me about Frost. Her eyes had been so bright. Sometimes they had that kind of sparkle when she talked about my poetry, and my heart knew I'd lost the only person who ever believed in me.

Holding onto the book, I opened my eyes. I looked at the pictures on the wall, wondering if Pru and her mom had met in heaven like the minister said. It seemed the only way I could breathe, believing they might've found each other there.

While I stood by all her books, the door to Pru's bedroom opened. My mom peeked her head in. She looked worried.

"Hi, Honey," she said. "I saw you come up here." She waited, while I put the book back up on Pru's shelf and went to sit on the bed. "Can I join you?"

I shrugged. She left the door open and walked in. "So this is Pru's room." She didn't sound sure, like maybe it wasn't anymore. Or maybe that's how I felt. "I guess you spent a lot of time here."

I shrugged again. "Yeah."

She stood as close to me as she dared. I hadn't been very easy the last few days. "I just want you to know, Jamie, that you can talk to me." Her words sounded sincere, but even if I thought she had time to listen, what would I say? How could I explain the loss in my heart? And how the hole left there felt like a forever-ness that could never ever be filled up with anything other than Pru.

"Okay," I whispered, staring at Pru's bedspread.

"I mean it, Jamie." She sat down next to me and put her arm around my shoulder. My mom wasn't big on affection, so I didn't know how to act. "I know this is a very hard thing. And you're so young." She pulled at my face with her hand, brushing my hair back. "But please don't keep it bottled up inside. Okay?"

I nodded and had a sudden desire to throw my arms around her. But I didn't. My arms felt like bricks, sinking me…taking me down. I just watched her move off the bed and give me a long look from the door. I gave her as much of a smile as I could. "I'm all right, Mom. I'll be down in a minute."

I stayed a little longer, just sitting there, waiting— for what, I didn't know. I kept taking deep breaths, trying to smell her, wanting one last piece of her to take with me. I needed something of Pru's. To hold onto. But what would be enough? Nothing really, except maybe the Robert Frost collection. And it seemed better, somehow, that it stay on her shelf.

When I came downstairs, Maxine walked over and handed me a plate of food. "I thought you might be getting hungry," she said, her arm around my shoulder. "Come sit down. You've been running around here all day, taking care of everything. Why don't you eat something. I got you a couple of those mini hot dogs you like."

I didn't know my sister to be so nice, and I let her lead me to the couch. She sat me down and put the plate on my lap, then went to the dining room, bringing me back a glass of lemonade.

"Thanks," I said.

I must've looked pretty bad by then because my parents started talking in low voices and then came to sit on either side of me on the couch. "Honey," my mom said. "Don't you think we should be going home? You've had a really long, emotional day."

I didn't answer. How could I tell her that I didn't know how to leave? That my legs didn't know how to walk out the Wheeler's front door. Because I was afraid I'd never be back. But I think Maxine understood I wasn't ready. She took the plate from me and put it on the coffee table. "I know you wanted to talk to Mr.

Wheeler and Marty," she said, taking me by the hand. "I think I saw them on the patio. Come on. Let's go see if they're free."

Again, I let her lead me. "Thanks," I said, feeling for the first time that Maxine was treating me like a person, not her little sister.

When Mr. Wheeler saw me, he stood and pulled me close, hugging me for a long time. When he finally let go, he had tears in his eyes. "I wanted to thank you, Jamie." He waved his hand in the air. "But there've been so many people. Your poems today—they were beautiful. Perfect really. You captured Pru just right. What you wrote was very special. I hope you'll let me have copies."

"Thanks Mr. Wheeler, and sure, you can have copies. And—and I'm really really sorry—you know, about Pru." It seemed an empty thing to say, knowing everyone at the house had probably said the same thing to him.

"You're a good friend, Jamie. The first real friend Pru ever had. I'm glad we all had a chance to know you. I hope you'll still come by and say hello from time to time. Don't forget us." He tried to smile, but it wouldn't quite come to his lips.

I needed to say something else to him, but the words came harder. "Mr. Wheeler—I—I also wanted to say how sorry I—am—about your—well, your wife.

Pru told me about her. She sounded really nice."

Mr. Wheeler's eyes blinked in surprise. Then he hugged me again, and I could feel him holding back some pretty big sobs, tears from deep inside. "Thank you. The wild columbine was an extra special touch," he said. "I loved having them there with the violets you brought Pru." When he drew back, he wiped his eyes. "Please, Jamie. Don't be a stranger."

I saw Marty alone in the backyard then, and even though it seemed maybe he wanted to be alone, I walked out to him. He stood off to one side of the lawn, staring out into the big field behind the house. "Marty?"

He turned, his face blank. Marty looked like he wanted to die but was being forced to live. He managed a small smile when he saw me. "Hi, Jamie."

"I—I uh, I just wanted to say goodbye. I said goodbye to your dad. I—I hope you guys are gonna be okay."

But they wouldn't be. Not for a long time. It's something you knew. Stuff like this just didn't get fixed overnight. "I'll stop by in a few days—you know, to check in. If you need anything, just call." The words sounded stupid, like Marty had a cold, and if I stopped over with some chicken noodle soup, he'd feel better.

"I'm glad you came out here, Jamie. I have something for you." His voice sounded like he'd cried himself out, with nothing left in him.

"For me?" It didn't seem like a day for gifts.

He nodded. "I thought you should have this." And with a quick and final look at his hand, Marty pulled Pru's ring off his pinky finger. "Here." He held it out in his palm.

I stared at the ring in horror—the beautiful ring from Pru's mom. The one Pru had worn every day. The one she cherished. I couldn't move. My hand didn't know how to reach out and take it from him.

When Marty saw my face, he moved closer to me, and just then, a little breeze blew between us, almost like Pru had sighed quietly, telling me to go ahead. I felt her there, and I think Marty felt it, too. Because he took my hand and placed the ring in my palm, closing my fingers over it. "Please take it. Pru would want you to have it."

Now, I don't know if I believed that. Being a best friend didn't mean you were entitled to family heirlooms or anything. And this—her mother's ring— well, it just didn't seem right. I blinked at the tears that started to come. All the words I had were stuck in the back of my throat along with that golf ball I'd never been able to get rid of.

"Mom would want you to have it." He let go of my hand and rubbed his pinky where the ring had been.

Marty's dark eyes, so like Pru's, told me no one else should have it but me. "I know you don't need a ring to remember Pru." His voice cracked. "But it would make me feel better knowing her best friend is wearing it."

Finally, I nodded. Slipping the ring onto my middle finger, I reached up and hugged Marty. Our tears mixed together as he kissed me on the cheek.

I thought maybe I really should leave then. Everyone looked tired—worn out and so sad. But as I walked back into the house to gather up my parents and tell them we could go, I had the horrible feeling that maybe I would become a stranger—that I already had. And that somehow Pru would become one, too. Someone I'd barely remember. Someone who'd meant so much to me, but would be a distant light, lost forever, swallowed in the stars.

Chapter 23
My Mom

I went back to school a week later. My three-day Memorial weekend had turned into an eight-day nightmare. And in that time, the world had changed and dumped my life in a big heap—everything turned upside down.

School seemed stupid—*everything* seemed stupid. Nothing mattered, and being in class without Pru felt like a weather report predicting rain all day. If people tried to talk to me, I answered without looking at them.

When Ms. Woods excused us for recess, I stayed in my seat, not wanting to go outside. Not wanting to do anything—not without Pru. Ms. Woods sat down next to me after the kids left class. "Jamie," she said, with a gentle voice. "You can spend recess inside today if you'd like. You can read or work quietly."

"Thanks Ms. Woods."

"But I want you to know that since you've been out, none of the kids have been playing lacrosse. I was hoping that when you came back, you'd keep the game going."

I blew air out of my cheeks in a long sigh. "Gosh, Ms. Woods, I don't know if I can." It seemed a thousand years since I'd played lacrosse.

"Well, I hope you'll consider it. The boys have already been asking, and it would be a nice tribute to Pru—to preserve what you and she worked on together."

I told her I'd think about it.

That night, I asked to be excused early from dinner, knowing that if I had to look for one more minute at the burned meatloaf and lumpy mashed potatoes my mom had made for a special "almost summer vacation dinner," I might explode. Or die.

Sprawled out on my bed, I stared at the ceiling, wondering what happened to Pru. It bothered me a lot. I felt lost and worried, thinking about God—hoping there was one who would keep Pru safe. In the history of sixth grade, there'd never been anyone so *little*. It would be easy for her to get lost in the crowd of people in heaven, if that's where she was.

I was thinking about Pru and where she'd gone, when somebody knocked at my door. I guess my not answering meant 'come in' because my mom stuck her head in and then leaned against the door frame. She held a plate of food. "I made you a bologna sandwich, Jamie. I know you weren't hungry at dinner."

Mom knew my all-time favorite sandwich and that I probably wouldn't be able to resist. But she didn't push. She just reached in and put the plate down on my desk. "Do you feel like talking?" she asked.

The Power of Two

I almost gave my usual 'no,' when I remembered what Pru had said, about not waiting—to talk to my mom before it was too late. And I felt shaky then, thinking how fast Pru had died, and what if my mom or dad or Maxine just disappeared the way she had. So, without inviting my mom in, I sat up and decided to try. I blurted out the thing that had been on my mind all night. "It feels stupid to be at school now."

I expected my mom to give a speech—keep my chin up and that things would get better in time, and how I had to think of summer vacation as a new start. All stuff I'd heard Pru's relatives say to her brothers after the funeral. But instead, my mom walked over to the bed and sat down.

"I'm not going to tell you it's going to be okay, Jamie." She paused, tracing the pattern in my bed quilt with her finger. "Because I don't think it will be. Not for a long time."

"Everything seems stupid." The words welled up in me like a volcano, ready to spew out something ugly. "Really damn stupid."

My mom nodded, like it didn't matter that I'd said a swear word. I'd felt like swearing a lot since Pru died, and I thought there might be more words ready to come out any minute. My mom turned to me. "I suspect things will feel really *really* damn stupid for a while."

I stared at my mom, surprised. And just as I started

to say how scared I felt to go to school without Pru, her cell phone rang. Right away, I could feel myself shut down, expecting her to take the call and hurry out of the room. But instead, she pulled the phone from her pocket and turned it off without even looking at the caller ID.

It took me a minute to get over the shock of seeing my mom *not* answer her phone. But she waited for me, not rushing. Finally, I said, "Ms. Woods wants me to start up the lacrosse team again."

I expected some rah rah talk about that being a good idea, but again, my mom surprised me. "It seems like that would be a really hard thing to do."

I started to cry. Big, giant sobs that a steamroller couldn't have stopped. "I don't know where Pru is!" I whispered into a Kleenex I'd pulled from a box by my bed. "I don't know if she's in heaven or if there *is* a heaven." I sobbed then, out of control, my words mixed in with a lot of blubbering. I blew my nose and tried to stop crying, but tears just kept coming and coming. "Where is she, Mom? Where's Pru?"

My mom turned and pulled me to her then, and I let her, falling into her arms like water. And that's when she said the best thing in the world—the only thing that finally calmed me down and helped me sleep that night.

"She's wherever you want her to be, Jamie." She rocked me, like when I had the flu, and I hugged her chest, tighter and tighter, holding on like she might leave, too. "I think she'll be in the flowers—violets for sure—and in the sunlight, like the poem you wrote." She spoke soft, next to my ear, words that were only for me. "And I think she'll be in the trees and at the pond and in every night sky you look to. She'll be everywhere. Anywhere. Whenever you want her to be."

Lori J. Sawicki

Chapter 24
The Big Confrontation

When Dad dropped me off at school the next morning, I still hadn't decided about playing lacrosse. I brought the t-shirts to class just in case, but I dreaded recess.

When the bell rang, the boys came to my desk. "Are we going to play?" Matt chewed on a fingernail, and Aaron looked hopeful. "Do you think we can get some more t-shirts? A few kids from the other classes want to join in."

Their questions upset me because they didn't seem to notice that Pru was gone. And I wanted to point out that half the original team was missing. To ask why they didn't care. But I just took a deep breath and nodded, feeling a little panicked as I went to my locker.

Pulling out the equipment and the box with the slips of paper felt like a betrayal to Pru, and it made a bigger rip in my heart. But everyone seemed excited to play again, and some kids from the other classes mobbed me with questions. So I kept going, though I didn't want to. Alone had never felt so big.

Matt and Aaron were good at the game now, so they helped teach the new kids who'd never played. Watching them, I knew how happy Pru would've been, seeing everybody together—like a *team.*

Everybody, that is, except for Sadie and the TCs. They stood off at the side, in their huddle, sometimes whispering, sometimes watching. For the rest of the week, that's all they did. It's like they were waiting for something. And I knew whatever was coming…it was bad. Really bad. And I wasn't sure I could face it. Not without Pru.

And then on Friday, Sadie made her move. She walked out to the field wearing a bright red shirt, the word CAPTAIN across the front in black letters. All the TCs wore red shirts, too, with ASSISTANT on theirs. They looked like a giant strawberry moving toward me. And they seemed to have a lot of support because some girls from other classes who'd never asked to play followed behind them.

So that was it. That's what the huddle was about. A takeover. Sadie probably worked out all the details when Pru died, and I was out of school. The thought of it made me shiver. But I think even more, it made me mad.

And right then, when Sadie walked over to the bench with the TCs in her shadow, all of them acting smug, heading into their huddle again, I stopped being scared. They giggled. And whispered. But it all felt sort of stupid—like school, like everything. Living through the death of your best friend, well, it changes your idea of what's worth being afraid of, that's for sure.

Each TC moved to the box and picked a position,

and the new kids did the same. For the first time since Pru and I started the lacrosse team, we didn't have enough equipment. More and more kids from the other classes wanted to play. So, it meant we'd all have to take turns sitting out. When Matt and I stopped to talk about the best way to do that, Sadie used it to her advantage. She stood by the bench and confronted me, her eyes dark and hard.

"So, Jamie. This is all really confusing." She talked loud, getting the kids' attention. I turned to face her, feeling one of those swear words just beneath my tongue. "I mean, if everybody in our class is going to play, and kids from other classes, *too,* and we don't have enough equipment, we're going to waste time every recess—stopping, switching positions, sharing t-shirts." She paused, waving her hand in the air like the whole world might end if we played that way. "I think we should pick teams. And stick to them. Everyone on the team should have the same position every day."

The girls beside her nodded in agreement, and I knew the rest. Sadie wanted a leader. She wanted to *be* the leader. This wouldn't be finished until the light was shining back in her corner.

"But then not everyone could play," I said. I was able to hold back a shiver that wanted to go crawling over my skin. I'd never heard the playground so quiet.

"Well, the new kids will just have to sit out because they didn't play in the beginning. They can watch and learn." She said this like it made perfect sense to exclude at least ten kids. That it made no difference at all.

I looked over at those ten kids who listened to us with big, worried eyes. You could tell they wanted someone to defend them.

"But I think they'd all like to play." When I said it, a lot of heads bobbed up and down.

"And why don't we pick two captains," Sadie went on, like she didn't hear me. Again, the TCs agreed. "I think it'll just be easier to handle everything during recess." She tossed her head, her braids flinging behind her shoulders.

I felt big anger inside. I could see through her Saran Wrap. Sadie thought I'd become a bird with a broken wing or a boat without one of its oars. That without Pru, I had no power. That what we'd done as two, couldn't possibly go on as one. That I'd become weaker now.

And even if I did feel weak, I knew how disappointed Pru would be if I let Sadie undo everything we'd worked for. Making a real team. Where everyone could play. The yuck feeling came back, and it came fast.

All the words I wanted to say were trapped in my heart with the biggest sadness in the history of the world. And when I didn't answer right away, Sadie started in about how to pick captains, and how there needed to be a girl captain. Because it wouldn't be fair without one. All the kids talked at once, alarm in their voices. And that's when one word managed to break away and come to the surface. A word I wasn't familiar with, and one that I'm sure Sadie didn't know at all.

"No."

My one word speech didn't come out very loud, but it's all I had. And maybe, it's all I had to say. Everybody shut up. More silence filled the playground. The kids looked at Sadie, then at me. Sixth grade waited.

Sadie seemed to puff up then, pulling her shoulders back and sticking out her chest like a big-time wrestler. She looked kind of stupid, and instead of being afraid, I laughed.

The TCs gasped, and Sadie tried hard not to look embarrassed. "Well," she said, looking at all the kids around us, "I say yes."

And there it was. The biggest standoff in the history of sixth grade. The most popular girl facing off with the girl at the bottom—the disease. Aunt Judy's cake. It seemed like the biggest moment for all of us. For me, especially.

Did you ever hear someone say they'd reached a fork in the road? My dad had been saying it a lot when he talked about his job at Corman Realty. I stared at Sadie's wormy, brown eyes and understood what that meant. I didn't need a dictionary or Pru to explain it. I was about to take a new path—one that led me away from the TCs forever. A path that had no railings to hold onto.

"No," I said again. "It's fine the way it is."

Sadie's dark eyes fired up, and it looked like her volcano would erupt. The TCs pulled back, and I knew I'd started down the path, all by myself.

Just as Sadie stepped forward, her eyes all squinty and her fists clenched like she might hit me, Matt helped end it. His words came out simple. Easy. "I agree with Jamie. It's fine the way it is." He paused, brushing a flop of hair from his forehead. "Everybody can take turns on the bench. We'll figure out the rest later."

The boys clapped with a big "Yes!" Someone yelled, "Jamie's right! Come on, let's play!" because no one wanted to waste time standing around talking about it. The new kids started to breathe again, and everyone ran out onto the field, leaving Sadie behind. She stood, mouth open, nothing coming out, not knowing how to save her commander status. She was speechless.

I put on my shirt, thinking that Pru would be extra happy for the way things were turning out. Right then, a tiny breeze blew against my cheek. It moved in and around my face. It pushed at my bangs. I closed my eyes and took a deep breath, and then another. I swear I could smell purple in the air. Something. Something Pru-like. And I remembered what my mom had said to me.

Opening my eyes, I looked up. A single cloud floated in the sky—a cloud with gold and lavender edges. It didn't move. It was one small puff hanging there like the sun or moon. I stared at it a long time. And right then, I was able to breathe. Just a little.

The breeze came again, and the cloud began to move away. I watched it go, giving a tiny Pru-nod to myself. "Okay," I said to no one, whispering the words. "Okay."

I almost had a smile in my heart that morning, though it would take many more weeks before it ever reached my lips. But as I followed the others out onto the field, I knew my days as a lemming had ended. And wherever I stood—middle, bottom, or some place else—it didn't matter anymore. The taste of Aunt Judy's chocolate cake had disappeared.

Lori J. Sawicki

Chapter 25
The Last Poem

Being back at school still felt mostly awful. I missed Pru, and my stomach rolled around in a sick way every morning until lunchtime, when I somehow choked down my bologna sandwich. I still had Loser Syndrome, I guess, because I sat by myself. But one day, some girls from other classes who'd asked to play lacrosse invited me to eat with them. So, that made things a little bit okay.

Most days, I wanted to be by myself, curled up in bed. But I could forget that ever happening—not with the Wheatland Miss Teen Pageant coming up. Our house had turned back into the Corman Zoo.

Some of Maxine's friends came over to help quiz her on questions the judges might ask and give their final opinions on her dress, hair, and makeup. Constant yakking went on along with a million calls for me to "Come quick!" and "Help find my necklace," and "Tweets! Have you seen my cell phone?!"

I spent most of the weekend in my room, my door shut to all the Maxine-attention. It seemed that everybody had forgotten about Pru. Her star had already faded in the sky. During those days, no one understood how I felt...how the forever-ness of missing Pru kept sweeping me away.

That weekend, I wrote a lot of poetry. Most of it

sounded sad, no rhymes—the pages refused to take any happy or hopeful words. By Sunday night, after Maxine had interrupted me a million more times to help find her black shoes, and then the slip with the slit up the back, not the one with the lace, I hurled my spiral notebook across the room in frustration, watching it slam into the closet door and land with a splat on the carpet. It was open to the last page, and that's when I saw the poem.

Now, I'd only half filled that notebook. But from where I sat, I could see the final page had a poem written on it. I walked over and turned it right-side up, having that feeling when you think someone's watching you, but you know no one's there. I stared at the poem, then sat down on the floor to read it. A poem from Pru.

More Than a Sunflower
Hidden in the shadow
of a tall, endless flower
you feel alone
without power
beneath the shade
of what grows so high
you feel lost in the darkness
no sun from the sky.
But never regret
Not being a flower
Because you're more than that

The Power of Two

you're a meteor shower!

To my best friend Jamie, Love, Pru

I read the poem, again and again, swiping at tears that fell in puddles on the paper. And then I hugged the notebook to my chest and laid on the floor, my knees pulled up tight against me. I knew she'd written it after our day at the pond, when I told her about Maxine and feeling like a weed next to a beautiful sunflower. And she'd said, with her Pru-wisdom, "You probably don't feel like you get any sun." And I'd looked at her, surprised, but not surprised, because she always understood me.

I cried hard that night, knowing I'd never have Pru or any of her Pru-wisdom again. And as much as I loved her poem—loved that she'd put it there to surprise me someday—it just didn't seem enough. Not enough to keep me going for the rest of my life.

****

The night of Maxine's pageant, I begged my parents to let me stay home. But Mom said she thought the entire family should be there to show support. Mostly, I think she just wanted me to come out of my room, which is where I stayed most of the time.

We sat on bleachers in the Wheatland football stadium where they held the pageant if it didn't rain. A stage was set up in the middle of the field with chairs for the judges in front. All the girls had on long, beautiful dresses, sparkly necklaces, and more lipstick than they needed. Like my sister, they probably all had their own TCs to make them look gorgeous.

I worked my way through a bag of popcorn that tasted like Styrofoam and yawned when the final competition took place—when the girls got up in front of the microphone to answer a question from the judges. A lot of their answers seemed pretty silly, but then so did the questions, even though the judges tried to make them sound important. I was losing interest by the time Maxine walked to the front of the stage in the black dress that Pru had loved so much.

"Maxine Corman," a voice said. "Every day, the media is filled with people who are portrayed as heroes. Who would you say has had the biggest influence on your life—who would you say has been a hero for you?"

I rolled my eyes, thinking Maxine would give one of her speeches about Hillary Clinton or some world leader. And I immediately tuned out, popping another piece of Styrofoam in my mouth. I didn't care to hear it. She yakked on this topic all the time.

But just when I thought I couldn't eat one more kernel of popcorn, I heard my name.

At first, the words seemed to come from far away,

like maybe Pru had spoken to me from heaven, and my heart lurched around like a pinball. But when my mom elbowed me in the side, I blinked back into focus to hear Maxine talking about me from the stage.

"Now, you might not think a little sister could be your hero," she went on. "But Jamie has been mine for a long time." She paused, looking out into the crowd, like she wanted to find me. "She keeps everything together. Every*one* together. But especially me."

The pinball action in my chest moved at super-speed. Had she really said that about me? This didn't sound like the same person who lived down the hall from me at home. "She makes calm out of chaos. And the one thing my sister knows how to do best, is help people. I'll give you an example."

As I listened, a hundred cotton balls puffed up in my throat. My mom put her arm around me, hugging me close. I could feel her smiling.

"My sister recently lost her best friend. She died suddenly, and her family was devastated. Not only did my sister give a eulogy at the funeral—the most beautiful, touching, eloquent speech from an eleven-year-old—she spent the afternoon taking care of her friend's family at the luncheon that followed. She brought them cold drinks, tried to get them to eat, greeted people at the door, and made sure the table was always filled with food. I watched her do this all day. She knew *exactly* what to do. And she's only eleven."

"When I saw the kind of love she showed for the family, and how easy it was for Jamie to somehow know the right thing to do, I found myself even more in awe of her than I usually am. That's why I count on her so much to help me. I ask her to be there to do things I know no one else can."

"Jamie knows how to help people," she went on. "To calm down, to stop crying, to stop being stressed, and to believe that everything will turn out all right. She's always done those things for me." She paused again, like she wanted to make her words clear. "I don't think it takes running into a burning building or saving a drowning man to be a hero. Sometimes—maybe most of the time—it just takes being a friend."

The crowd broke into applause—loud and thundering—and I sat there stunned as my sister walked back to her seat. My mom and dad yelled, "Yeah Maxine!" from their places on either side of me, and I sat in silence between them. I had no idea my sister had ever, in the history of my entire life, felt that way about me.

Maxine, of course, won the pageant. She stood on stage, smiling that giant, sunflower smile of hers, while last year's winner placed a sparkly crown on her head. I couldn't help but think of Pru then, and how much she would've loved seeing it. How she would've said "that's beeeuuuttiful," hinting that she'd like to try it on. I touched the purple ring on my finger and felt happy and very sad at the same time.

The Power of Two

My sister walked the stage with the crown on her head, and I found myself clapping along with the rest of the crowd, amazed to think that Maxine loved me enough to call me a hero. Aside from meeting Pru, it was the best surprise of my life. My sister looked really happy, and so I decided to be happy for her, too. With a glance to the sky, I wondered if Pru was watching. If the sparkle from Maxine's crown had made it all the way to the stars.

Lori J. Sawicki

Chapter 26
A Purple Feeling

Afterward, we went to dinner at a restaurant with all the girls in the pageant. I didn't really want to go. I hadn't felt like doing much of anything for a long time, and eating out together just made me remember Pru and the kiwi lemonade. But I didn't say anything. This was Maxine's night, and she'd made a nice speech about me. It seemed the least I could do was go along without a fuss.

When we got to the restaurant, all the girls crowded around my sister. They hugged her, not acting upset or jealous at all that she'd won. I watched them while we waited for our table, missing Pru like crazy. But then Maxine did another surprising thing: she stepped out of their huddle and grabbed my hand, pulling me into the group.

Now, I know I should've been happy for the attention, and that my sister had included me in her circle, but there I stood again—in the middle. Only this time, I stood in the center of a huge bouquet of sunflowers. Their beauty put me in shadows, blocking the light, making me invisible. But that's when Maxine introduced me.

"This is Jamie," my sister said. "The hero I talked about."

All the girls who didn't know me shook my hand,

and everybody smiled like I'd become someone special—not just Maxine's little sister. One of the girls gave me a wink and said, "Well, after a speech like that, maybe *Jamie* should be wearing the crown tonight!" And all the girls laughed and patted me on the back.

Maxine's eyes sparkled. "You know, Stef, I think you're right." And then she reached up and took the crown from her head, pulling the little combs from her hair. She gave it a long look, then put the crown on me. "I think it fits better on Jamie anyway."

For a second, I felt alone in that very crowded restaurant. Has that ever happened to you? There are lots of people around, but you don't see them or hear them? Odd sounds plug up your ears and the room blurs? That's how I felt right then—like I didn't know my real life or remember the person I'd been just a few hours before. This new path had taken me to a new place, and there I was, beginning to see it for the first time.

Everything I'd known for sure felt far behind me. I could only stand there with my mouth open, which seemed to be the way I dealt with a lot of things that year. When I finally found my voice, I reached up and started to pull the crown from my head. "This is yours, Maxine," I said. "You should wear it."

But she put her hand over mine and stopped me, shaking her head with the softest smile I'd ever seen. "No. You wear it tonight—if you want to. You deserve it."

In those moments, with Maxine's hands clasped over mine, each of us holding onto that crown, I thought about all the surprises of the past few weeks: Pru telling Marty I was the best person she'd ever known; finding Pru's poem; my mom being there when I needed her; standing up to Sadie; and now my sister calling me a hero. Nothing about the picture seemed familiar. Or maybe I just didn't recognize myself in it.

Everything was all mixed up. The new path felt crooked and filled with contradictions. A middle-girl suddenly a hero? Instead of a weed, a meteor shower? A loser standing up to a commander? Maybe I'd thought of myself as one thing for so long, I didn't know how to think of myself as something else.

But one thing I did know: Pru had taken me to a place I believed in more than where I'd been. And though I didn't know how my life would be without her, I knew I'd changed because of her.

And I knew another thing for sure: Pru would've wanted me to wear the crown. She would've said something like, "It's your turn in the sun, Jamie. You're not in the shade anymore." Strange, I felt the purple again—right then, with Maxine's hand on my head. A kind of swirling, a drifting of some small gust of air that floated in between us. Filled with color. I don't know, maybe I just wanted it to be. But I swear, purple moved all around me.

So, with a Pru-like nod, I let Maxine put the crown on my head, and I left it there—all the way through dinner, and up until I went to bed. Though my family might've thought I wore the crown that night for me, I really wore it for Pru. In honor of the person who'd pulled me down a new path and helped me walk on it without being scared. And for a friendship that taught me that meteor showers were brighter than sunflowers—you just had to look longer sometimes to see them. I wore Maxine's crown that night for the best friend in the history of the entire world.

THE END

ABOUT THE AUTHOR

I started writing fiction in elementary school, plunking out my stories on an old Underwood typewriter my dad bought at an auction. They were mysteries, mostly, because of my love for 'Trixie Belden' and 'Nancy Drew' books—stories that would take me away for an entire Saturday afternoon.

My fifth grade teacher let me stay in at recess and use his typewriter to work on my fiction. When I finished, I'd tie my pages together with turquoise binky yarn. After all these years, I still have those stories.

Throughout my career, and in all my jobs, I stayed close to words. I spent years as a technical writer and documentation manager, and I taught technical writing and English at Eastern Michigan University. But in whatever spare time I had, I was always writing fiction. My first children's novel, *Because Sometimes a Miracle is a Pussy Willow Tree*, was published in 2002.

Currently, I'm employed as an online writing tutor for Smarthinking while working on additional Identity Novels. My second in this collection, *When Truth Puts Its Shoes On*, will be available this winter. Be sure to look for it! www.identitynovels.com

I live in Ann Arbor with my husband, Chuck, and our rescue dog, Shoobie. Chuck and I have a son, Nathan, who currently attends the University of Michigan.

Lori J. Sawicki

35266286R00113

Made in the USA
Middletown, DE
04 February 2019